'At least say *something*!'

Closing out the doubts, Claire brought up both hands and cupped them about the lean jaw, bringing Ross's head down to put her lips to his. Life was for living, she had told herself not so very long ago, so why not start living it?

'You're a regular bundle of surprises,' he growled softly.

'I'm fed up with being Miss Goody Two Shoes!'

'Goody Two Shoes never had a temper like yours. Small and fiery, yet totally unpredictable, too. I've a feeling you might turn out to be more than I can handle.'

Kay Thorpe was born in Sheffield in 1935. She tried out a variety of jobs after leaving school. Writing began as a hobby, becoming a way of life only after she had her first completed novel accepted for publication in 1968. Since then, she's written over fifty and lives now with her husband, son, German shepherd dog and lucky black cat on the outskirts of Chesterfield in Derbyshire. Her interests include reading, hiking and travel.

THE
WEDDING
DECEPTION

BY
KAY THORPE

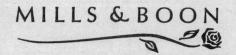

MILLS & BOON

All the characters in this book have no existence outside the imagination of the author, and have no relation whatsoever to anyone bearing the same name or names. They are not even distantly inspired by any individual known or unknown to the author, and all the incidents are pure invention.

*MILLS & BOON and the Rose Device
are trademarks of the publisher.
Harlequin Mills & Boon Limited,
Eton House, 18-24 Paradise Road, Richmond, Surrey TW9 1SR*

© Kay Thorpe 1995

ISBN 0 263 79383 4

*Set in Times Roman 10 on 11¼ pt.
01-9602-57823 C1*

Made and printed in Great Britain

CHAPTER ONE

WITH only half an hour to go before closing time, there was little chance of any more customers happening by, Claire reckoned. Not quite the worst day's trade she had known, but a very long way from being the best either.

The weather was the main culprit. There was little pleasure to be found in traipsing round the shops in the rain. June had been a total wash-out this year. Hopefully, July and August would be better. If not she was going to be left with a lot of summer stock on her hands—something she could ill afford.

Her neck still ached from bending over her account books for so long earlier. She ran a hand under the heavy curve of hair the colour of a new penny to ease her nape, grimacing a little. No matter how she totted up the figures, they told the same story—Candice was going steadily downhill.

It could do no harm to shut shop early for once, she decided, shelving her problems for the moment. Jill would be back from visiting her friend in Buxton by now, and would no doubt be hungry. It was too much to hope that she would have taken it on herself to prepare a meal, of course. Cooking simply wasn't her forte, as she was fond of pointing out.

When it came to housework of any kind, little was, Claire reflected with fond humour. It wasn't exactly her own favourite pastime either, but she couldn't find it in herself to resent her sister's easy assurance that all would be provided. With A levels behind her, Jill had a right to a few weeks of self-indulgence before going on to university.

Ideally, her grades would be good enough to secure her the place at Warwick already on offer, although she had spent far too many evenings out with friends when she should have been studying for the exams, in Claire's estimation. With only six years between the two of them, laying down the law didn't come easy.

About to turn over the 'Closed' sign in the glass door, she felt her heart give a sickening jerk as a man loomed in the doorway. Only a couple of weeks ago the lady in children's wear next door had been subjected to an attack by some man not yet apprehended by the police. Her personal injuries had been more emotional than physical, but he had got away with the day's takings and had left the woman afraid to be on her own in the shop.

This one hardly looked the type to be contemplating robbery, she thought in swift self-reassurance, assessing the expensive cut of his light wool jacket and immaculately pressed beige trousers. Hardly the type to patronise an establishment such as this either, but he could be in search of something for his wife, she supposed.

'I was just about to close,' she said, opening the door, 'but you're welcome to come in and take a look around if you like.'

'You're Claire Marcroft?' he asked shortly.

'Well, yes.' She was disconcerted both by his use of her name and by his tone. 'How can I help you?'

Already inside the shop, he cast an appraising glance over the place before turning back to meet her questioning green eyes. He topped her by a good six inches or more despite her high heels. His eyes were grey, she noted fleetingly, their regard somehow discomfiting. A stray shaft of sunlight, angling in through the window, picked up a healthy glint in his thick dark hair. The hard-boned, essentially masculine features were vaguely familiar.

'Is there somewhere we can talk?' he said.

'There's the office,' she acknowledged. 'But I don't see what——'

'Supposing we go there?' he interrupted.

'Supposing you tell me what it is you're here for first,' Claire rejoined crisply, recovering some degree of composure. 'Mr...?'

'Laxton,' he supplied. 'Ross Laxton.' He watched her expression change, an ironic line to his mouth. 'I see the name means something to you.'

'There was an article about you in the local paper a few weeks ago,' she confirmed. 'And a photograph. You're head of HR Incorporated.'

'No other connection?'

She hesitated, doubtful whether someone in his position should be making such a call, and unable to think of a reason. 'Is it to do with the lease?'

'I don't deal with leases.' His tone was dry.

'No, of course not.' Claire was embarrassed by the gaffe. 'It's just that with the company owning this whole row of shops, and my lease due for renewal soon, I thought...' She left it there, aware of stating the obvious, and said instead, 'So what exactly is it you *are* here for?'

He took his time replying, studying the clean lines of her face with its wide-spaced eyes, small straight nose and generously curved mouth. She could feel herself growing warm beneath the scrutiny, and hoped that the flush didn't show. No doubt she didn't begin to compare with the women a man of his looks and kind was accustomed to viewing at such close quarters, but that was no reason for him to look quite so disparaging.

'Are you and your sister very much alike?' he asked, startling her because it was the last thing she had expected him to say.

'Only superficially,' she found herself answering, before catching herself up. Brows drawn together, she started to ask how he knew that she had a sister, but he forestalled her.

'Your parents are dead, I understand.'

Claire swallowed on the sudden hard lump in her throat, caught unawares by the bald statement. Even after all this time the pain was still like a spear through her heart.

'They were killed in a car crash four years ago,' she said with control. 'Although I fail to see what business it is of yours.'

'You were how old at the time?' he continued, ignoring the latter remark.

'Twenty.' The reply was dragged from her against her will. 'I really don't see——'

'Hardly mature enough to be left in total charge of a fourteen-year-old, would you say? Especially in this day and age.'

'There was no one else.' She was fast losing the little tolerance remaining in her. 'Will you please tell me what this is all about?'

The dark head inclined, its lean features set in uncompromising lines. 'As your sister doesn't appear to have told you herself, it seems I have to do it for her.' He paused briefly. 'To put it bluntly, she's pregnant.'

Shock kept Claire both motionless and speechless for several seconds. She could only gaze at him with eyes gone wide and dark. When she did find her voice at last, it sounded totally unlike her own.

'You must have got the wrong person!'

He gave a short, humourless laugh. 'I doubt if there are two Jill Marcrofts in town with sisters who run a boutique on High Street.'

Mind whirling, she said thickly, 'Are you claiming to be the father?'

His lips thinned. 'I'm not in the habit of playing around with girls almost half my age.'

'Then who is supposed to be?' she demanded, even more confused.

'My younger brother,' he said. 'With "supposed" very much the operative word.'

'Just a minute!' Claire wasn't too far gone to recognise the imputation. 'You're saying my sister is pregnant but your brother isn't the one responsible?'

'I'm saying there's room for doubt.'

'You get out of here!' Face hot, eyes sparking like twin emeralds, she only barely stopped herself from smashing her hand across the lean brown cheek. 'Just get out!'

If he recognised the danger of a physical attack, he wasn't allowing it to deter him. He made no move, but simply stood there looking at her with infuriating condescension.

'As the bearer of bad news, I'd hardly expect to be greeted with open arms, but it does none of us any good to fly off the handle. The sooner you face up to it, the sooner we can start getting the whole sorry business sorted out.'

'There's nothing to sort out!' She forced the words between clenched teeth. 'I don't believe a word of it!'

The sigh held more than a hint of impatience. 'There appears to be little doubt about the pregnancy. It's Scott's involvement I'm here to discuss.' The very way he said the word 'involvement' underlined his rejection, as did the following, 'He's altogether too gullible.'

Claire drew in a long, slow breath, fighting to restrain her wilder impulses. It couldn't be true, she told herself. There simply had to be a mistake somewhere! *That* should be straightened out first.

'Assuming we're not talking about a single instance, just how long is this...affair supposed to have been going on?' she managed, with creditable steadiness.

Broad shoulders lifted in a brief shrug. 'According to Scott, since early May.'

'That makes it even less likely! Jill was still in school then.'

'In school, maybe, but not necessarily with her mind on her work. Anyway, why would he lie about it?'

'Never having met your brother, I've no idea what his motives might be,' she retorted tautly. 'All I am sure of is that if Jill really had been carrying on a relationship with him—or with anyone else, for that matter—I'd have known about it.'

The grey eyes registered scepticism. 'Are you trying to claim she never even had a boyfriend before?'

'Of course I'm not. She's a very pretty and popular girl.'

'So I'm given to understand.'

Her chin jerked up, her fists clenching involuntarily at her sides. 'Are you suggesting what I think you might be?'

'I'm suggesting,' he said, without change of tone, 'that you may not know your sister quite as well as you believe you do.'

She gazed at him in silence for a lengthy moment, grappling with the thought that if this story of his turned out to have any truth in it at all, then he might well be right. Jill had certainly been very moody recently. Claire had put it down to nervousness over her coming exam results, but this cast a whole new light on things. Pregnant! It didn't bear thinking about!

'Is your brother denying responsibility?' she asked, trying her best to maintain some semblance of composure.

Ross shrugged again. 'On the contrary, he's only too ready to accept what he believes *is* his responsibility, and do the right thing.'

'You mean...marriage?'

'Yes.'

'But obviously you don't agree?'

'He's only just twenty-two. The last thing he needs at this juncture is being lumbered with a wife and family.'

'I'd think him old enough to decide that for himself.'

The grey eyes were unrelenting. 'Old enough, maybe; sensible enough, definitely not. Anyway, it isn't just *his* future I'm concerned about. My father's already suffered one stroke. A shotgun wedding would just about finish him off completely.'

Claire made no attempt to offer meaningless sympathy. 'Do I take it you're the only one of the family your brother has confided in so far?' she got out.

'That's right,' Ross confirmed. 'He only told me about it a couple of hours ago. I decided it best to tackle you here on your own rather than come to the house.'

'Hoping for what?' she demanded, with a curl of her own lip. 'You've more or less accused my sister of being a promiscuous little tart. Did you expect me to confirm it for you?'

His face darkened, lips compressing. 'You're putting words into my mouth.'

'I don't think so. You've made your opinion pretty clear.' She drew in another steadying breath, feeling the sick churning inside her threatening to take over. 'Does your brother know you were coming here?'

He shook his head, expression unapologetic. 'I took it on myself to try sorting something out.'

'Such as what?' Claire demanded. 'An offer of money, maybe?'

From the look that flickered across the lean features, she had hit the nail on the head. Anger momentarily swamped all over emotions, and was held in check with the greatest difficulty.

'I think you'd better go,' she said, voice low and tight.

The strong mouth took on a wry line, as if in acknowledgment of a tactical error. 'All right, so money isn't necessarily the answer. But you'd surely agree that marriage under these circumstances isn't the best thing either?'

'I don't know what I think.' Claire was close to losing her grip altogether. 'I'm not even convinced of the basic fact yet. Why should I take your word for it?'

'It isn't my word, it's my brother's,' he said. 'He's hardly likely to make such a claim for fun!'

Claire doubted it too. What man would? She felt totally at sea.

'I'd suggest you go and confront your sister with it,' said Ross after a moment, watching her face. 'Tomorrow being Sunday, we'll all be available for discussion, I take it.' It was more statement than question. 'I imagine Scott has your address. We'll come over together in the morning and talk it through.'

Further protestation would be a waste of time and effort, Claire accepted. Her first priority was to get home and see Jill.

Ross had taken her agreement for granted, and was already turning away to open the door again. A fine figure of a man, that part of her brain still functioning on normal levels registered: shoulders broad and powerful, hips lean, legs long and straight. A man she might well have found vitally attractive under normal circumstances.

If what he had told her really did turn out to be true—
and there seemed little chance that it might not—then
where did they go from here? she wondered numbly. Jill
had her whole life ahead of her, and university just
around the corner. With or without marriage, she was
far too young to be a mother.

The rain had stopped some time before, although the
pavements were still wet when she got outside. Carrying
her raincoat, she locked the door securely, then walked
down to the side-street where she had parked the little
red Fiat Panda.

Six years old, the car was in far from pristine condition, but it was all she could comfortably afford to
run, along with all her other expenses. For once, the
ignition fired on the first time of asking.

Claire put the car into motion, trying to look at things
rationally. Willing though Scott Laxton might be to 'do
the right thing', as his brother had so scathingly put it,
marriage didn't have to be the only answer. Jill might
not even want to marry him. It wouldn't be easy bringing
up a child, but between the two of them they could cope.
At least there wasn't the same stigma attached to single
motherhood these days.

She was getting way ahead of herself, she conceded
wryly at that point. It might even turn out to be a false
alarm. She hoped so. Oh, God, how she hoped so!

Set right on the edge of the Derbyshire Dales, Rowsley
was normally awash with weekend traffic at this time of
year. Today there was little to mar her progress out to
the suburb where she and Jill still lived, in the house
they had once shared with their parents.

Insurance money and savings left by her father and
mother had taken care of the mortgage, and there had
been enough left over to start up the boutique. Claire
had sold off part of the over-large garden to the people
owning the plot next door, who had wanted to extend,

and this had served the dual purpose of providing a sum to invest for Jill's future educational expenses, and shrinking the garden to manageable proportions. Claire spent much of her spare time in it, and was justifiably proud of the result.

This evening she had no eyes for the colourful display fronting the white-walled house. She left the car standing on the drive and went straight indoors, gathering herself before opening the sitting-room door.

Jill looked up from the magazine which she was flicking through, her lovely, if somewhat wilful face wearing an unusually diffident expression.

'Hi,' she said. 'Had a good day?'

Still not certain of how best to approach the subject, Claire shook her head. 'Not very.' She hesitated, then decided that the only way was to go head in. 'I had a visit from Ross Laxton.'

If there had been any doubt left in her mind at all regarding the veracity of his accusation, it was instantly dispelled by the look which sprang into the younger girl's eyes.

'He had no right to interfere!' she exclaimed angrily. 'I was going to tell you myself tonight.'

Claire pushed a shaky hand through her hair, struggling to stay on top of her emotions. 'How come I never even knew you were seeing Scott Laxton? Why all the secrecy, Jill?'

Defiance took over from annoyance. 'Because I knew how you'd react. My A levels had to be top priority all the way through, didn't they? Never mind what *I* wanted!'

'I thought going on to university *was* what you wanted,' Claire defended.

'You never bothered to ask. You even decided which universities I should apply to.'

'We decided that together. You never once——' Claire broke off, taking a hold on herself. 'There's really no point in going into all that now, is there?' she said, on as level a note as she could manage. 'When did you discover you were pregnant?'

Some unreadable expression flickered across the smooth young features. 'A week or so ago.'

'There's no chance that you might be wrong?'

'I did two tests.'

'But you haven't been seen by a doctor yet?'

'Scott is arranging all that privately. We're going to be married, no matter what *anyone* says!' she added forcefully. 'We love each other.'

Claire sank into the nearest chair, searching her mind for some way of getting through the barriers that Jill was putting up against her. 'How did you meet in the first place?' was all she could come up with.

'Scott likes discos,' came the answer, as if that explained everything. 'He's a terrific dancer!'

A typical teenage accolade, thought Claire wryly, recalling a time when she might have considered such a talent of prime importance herself. Jill was still so young in many ways.

'Did you know he was going to tell his brother about all this?' she asked, and saw her sister's face cloud again.

'He said he was going to tell them all as soon as he got back this afternoon.'

'You were with him this morning?'

'Yes.' The defiance was back. 'He took me into Buxton, so I didn't lie.'

'And that makes everything hunky-dory, does it?' Claire caught herself up, recognising the futility of lashing out in that way. What was done was done. What remained was to make the best of the situation.

'I'm afraid his brother doesn't see marriage as the obvious answer,' she said on a quieter note. 'I'm not sure I do either.'

Jill sat up straighter, expression determined. 'It isn't your or his decision to make! We're both of an age to choose for ourselves!'

'Of an age, perhaps, but there are other factors to be taken into account.'

'Such as what?' On her feet now, face flushed, hazel eyes flashing green lights, Jill looked ready to take on all comers. 'You'd rather I got rid of it?'

'No, of course not.' Claire put everything she knew into keeping an even tone. 'There are other alternatives.'

'Like swelling the single-parent ranks, for instance?' Deeper in colour than Claire's, and falling straight as a die to her shoulders, Jill's hair swung as she shook her head emphatically. 'Scott wouldn't settle for that even if I would. He wants this baby. We both do!'

'You're too young to know *what* you want,' Claire protested. 'I'm sure Scott is too.'

'Scott isn't just a boy. He's twenty-two.' From the way she said it, it was obvious that that made him mature enough for anything in her estimation. 'If it's money you're worried about, you don't need to. He can well afford to get married. He has investments left him by his grandmother, as well as his company shares.'

'I hadn't even got that far,' Claire admitted. She hesitated, studying her sister's mutinous face. 'Do you think you'd feel the same way about him if he was just an ordinary, working man?'

'Of course I would! It's *him* I love, not the money!' Jill made a sudden small gesture of appeal. 'You'll like him too, Claire. I know you will!'

He would have to be vastly different from his brother to make her like him, Claire reflected—a thought which brought an unpleasant reminder of Ross's parting promise.

'Ross Laxton is coming here with him in the morning,' she said. 'I doubt that his attitude is going to change overnight.'

'Scott is coming over tonight,' countered Jill. 'He wants to meet you.'

'Having left you to do the telling on your own.'

'Only because I wanted it that way. He's no coward!'

'Oh, I'm sure he's a regular paragon!' Claire instantly regretted the tart remark. Whatever her opinion might turn out to be, Jill wasn't going to be swayed. All the same, she couldn't find it in herself to retract the words. 'What time are you expecting him?' she said instead.

Whatever her thoughts, Jill was keeping them to herself. 'I told him around seven. He won't have eaten, by the way. He's still living at home, and they don't have dinner till eight.'

Claire bit back the instinctive comment. It was gone half-past six now. She did a hasty mental review of their food stocks. There were half a dozen local rainbow trout in the freezer, presented to them by their neighbour, who owned fishing rights on the river. They could be cooked from frozen on the microwave's sensor setting without losing too much flavour.

She had made a salad before leaving for the shop that morning, and had prepared a pan of new potatoes ready for the hob, intending to grill some steak to go with them. With apple pie and cream to follow, and cheese if required, there should be enough.

'Then we'd better get moving,' she said, putting everything else aside for the moment. 'Perhaps you could start setting the table.'

'OK.' Jill got to her feet with an alacrity that brought a faint, ironic smile to her sister's lips. 'I'll fetch a cloth.'

They normally ate most meals at the kitchen table, where a cloth wasn't needed. Obviously it had to be the dining-room for Scott.

Claire left her to it, going through to the small but well-equipped kitchen to start on the meal. The trout would no doubt be a poor substitute for the kind of dinner served at the Laxton homestead, but she wasn't going to allow *that* to concern her. Unexpected visitors took pot luck.

Unexpected was certainly the word. She could still hardly credit that this was really happening. A bare hour or so ago all she'd had to worry about was finance!

The trout weren't all that large. She sprinkled all six with lemon juice and black pepper, added a few dots of butter, then covered the dish in cling film. The potatoes and fish should be ready about the same time; the apple pie they would eat cold. She briefly contemplated opening a bottle of wine, but decided that that might be overdoing things a little. This was hardly a celebration.

Jill had used the silver, she noted, when she went to check the small oak-beamed dining-room. She had also left off the cloth, laying the woven place-mats directly on the polished surface of the table and placing a vase of flowers from the sitting-room in the centre. It looked nice, Claire was bound to admit.

The sound of a car turning into the drive drew her eyes to the window. Long and silver, the Mercedes came to a stop behind her Panda, and the engine was switched off.

Claire felt her heart jerk painfully as the driver unfolded his length from the vehicle. Ross's arrival could only mean that Scott wasn't coming. Which left Jill where?

CHAPTER TWO

THE opening of the front passenger door and emergence of a younger man brought mingled emotions, with relief playing only a minor part. Judging from the resemblance between the two, this almost certainly *was* Scott.

The two men moved around opposite sides of the Panda to head for the door. Ross was the taller by a couple of inches, and the more substantial in build, his chest broad and solid beneath the thin white sweater. Clad in similar casual style, Scott looked distinctly boyish by comparison.

Claire stirred herself reluctantly to go out into the hall as the two of them passed the window. Whatever was to come had to be faced. The sound of the doorbell brought Jill out from the sitting-room.

'He's here!' she exclaimed unnecessarily. 'I'll let him in.'

'He's not alone,' Claire warned, and saw the light in her eyes fade a little. 'He has his brother with him.'

Jill rallied with surprising speed. 'Then we'll just have to set another place.'

There was food enough for four, Claire supposed, although she didn't see Ross Laxton sitting down quietly to dinner. There could only be one reason why he had elected to accompany his brother tonight instead of waiting until morning, and that was to see that he made no rash promises.

She stayed where she was in the hall as Jill went to open the door, preparing herself for the coming encounter. Marriage might or might not be the best solution, but if it really did turn out to be what both of them wanted then she would fight tooth and nail for their right to make that decision.

Jill's invitation to enter sounded astonishingly composed. With features less forceful all round than his brother's, though certainly no less eye-catching, Scott looked apologetic.

'Not my idea,' he disclaimed, with obvious meaning. 'Any more than this afternoon was my idea.'

'Mine entirely on both counts,' Ross confirmed. 'I saw no point in waiting till tomorrow.'

Claire ignored him, her attention focused on the younger man.

'I can't pretend to be happy about all this,' she said, 'but there's no point in railing at you about it either. We can talk over dinner. It's just about ready.' She added, with the intention of changing the conversation, 'Perhaps you'd prefer a sherry or something first?'

'We didn't anticipate anything,' said Ross, before Scott could answer. 'Certainly not a meal.'

'We usually eat around this time,' Claire responded shortly. 'I saw no reason to alter our routine.' She started to turn, adding over a shoulder, 'I'll need to lay another place at table. Take them through to the sitting-room, Jill.'

Safe in the dining-room, she took a moment to compose herself before going to the sideboard to get extra cutlery from the drawer. This wasn't going to be an easy encounter.

The mats were in a cupboard beneath the old oak trolley which her mother had picked up for a song at one of the house sales she had used to frequent. None of the furniture in the house was worth a great deal in terms of antiquity, but each and every piece had been collected with discernment. With one or two exceptions, the delft plates on the shelf had mostly come from local markets, their faded colours taking on new life in the soft evening light.

Her mother had loved this house from the moment she had seen it, she had always said. Both she and her father had been loving people altogether. They would have known how best to deal with all this.

That way lay depression, Claire warned herself, shutting off the images. It was up to her to handle the situation—with Jill's happiness the prime consideration. Let Ross Laxton beware!

The three of them were seated on opposite sides of the stone fireplace: Jill and Scott together on one two-seater sofa, holding hands with an air of defiance and Ross on the other, looking like a fish out of water. There were no drinks in evidence, and Claire wasn't about to ask again. In any case, she didn't want anything to spoil.

'If you'd like to come through, we may as well get started,' she said.

Ross was first on his feet, filling the room with his presence. 'Lead on,' he invited with a derisive glint in his eyes. 'Something smells very good, I must say!'

He was mocking her efforts to act normally, Claire reflected. Well, two could play that game. She gave him a bland little smile.

'I hope it tastes as good as it smells.'

'I'm sure of it,' he said. 'It wouldn't dare do otherwise.'

Jill and Scott were on their feet now, both of them obviously aware of the cross-current running between their respective siblings.

'This is really good of you, Claire,' said Scott. 'Especially considering the shock it must have been to have it sprung on you that way,' he added, with a glowering glance at his brother.

'I apologise,' proffered Ross smoothly. 'I was labouring under some degree of shock myself.'

Claire returned his gaze with determined containment. If he thought that such tactics would disarm her, he was mistaken. His intimation earlier that Scott might not be Jill's only sexual experience had cut too deep to be so easily dismissed.

'I'm sure you were,' she said. 'Shall we leave it at that for the moment, and go and eat?'

She led the way, sensing Ross at her back—a little too close for comfort. She placed him at the foot of the oblong table, opposite her own seat, with Jill and Scott on either side, where they could gaze into each other's eyes to their hearts' content. One only had to look at the pair of them to see that they both felt the same way. Scott came across so differently from what she had anticipated after meeting his brother. There was a resemblance in looks, perhaps, but no resemblance whatsoever in personality.

She made no apologies for the lack of a starter, but gave both men two trout apiece, leaving them to help themselves to potatoes and salad. The succulent pink-tinged flesh gave off a delicate aroma as Ross slid the skin aside and eased out the whole skeletal framework with an expertise that Claire could only envy. No matter how carefully she dissected trout, she almost always at some point managed to get bones in her mouth, and disposing of them politely in public posed quite a problem.

Conversation was desultory while they ate, most of it prompted by Ross himself. Claire regarded his overtures with suspicion, sensing an attempt to lull the lot of them into believing him reconciled to the situation. There was no way a man of his kind would have changed his views so radically in the space of a couple of hours. Which meant that the crunch was still to come.

Whatever his motives, he finished every last morsel of the trout, laying down his knife and fork with a sigh of what appeared to be genuine satisfaction.

'Congratulations,' he commented. 'Those were beautifully cooked!'

'All down to the microwave,' disclaimed Claire, unwilling to accept the compliment under false pretences. 'Modern technology has its uses.'

'Especially when unexpected guests turn up,' came the dry rejoinder. 'Congratulations anyway. Not everyone can time a microwave correctly.'

It had done that itself too, but she let it pass, seizing the initiative before he could take it from her. 'We're not here to talk about food, are we?'

'No, we're not.' Scott sounded abrupt. 'Stop playing around, Ross.'

Still fixed on Claire, the grey eyes gave little away. 'All right, so let's talk. Marriage aside, we can surely come to some other mutually agreeable arrangement.'

'If you mean money, you can keep it!' Jill burst out, face flaming. 'And if you're thinking I might agree to have an abortion, you can think again! Do you hear?'

'I imagine half the neighbourhood heard,' he replied with irony. 'Let's try and stay rational about it, shall we?'

'I already told you what we're going to do about it,' said Scott forcefully. 'I don't need your approval!'

His brother regarded him for a moment with brows drawn together. 'Have you thought about what it's going to do to Dad?'

'That's emotional blackmail, and you know it!' The younger man's eyes were bright with resentment. 'We don't have to tell him about the baby right away, if it comes to that—just that I'm going to be married.'

'And where exactly were you planning on getting married?'

Scott exchanged glances with Jill, as if seeking confirmation of a previous agreement. 'Registry Office, probably.'

Ross lifted a sardonic eyebrow. 'At the risk of sounding pedantic, it's Register not Registry. That aside, you think he isn't going to guess why? The stroke affected his motor responses, not his reasoning power. He can still add two and two.'

'Is another stroke imminent?' asked Claire. 'I mean, have the doctors actually said he mustn't be put under any kind of stress?'

'Where there's been one, there's always danger of another. Any fool knows that.'

She bit her lip, bound to acknowledge a degree of justification in the rebuttal. She had spoken without thinking, intent only on calming the situation. All the same, she had no intention of taking it lying down.

'You must win a lot of friends with that line,' she said, without attempting to mute the tartness.

Surprisingly, his lips twitched. 'A figure of speech. Nothing personal.'

Like hell! she thought.

Scott made a sudden impatient movement. 'Look, we're not getting anywhere like this.' He eyed Claire with determination in the line of his mouth. 'Are *you* on our side?'

She wasn't wholly, but neither was she prepared to join forces with his brother. 'Yes,' she said firmly.

His smile was brilliant, his whole face relaxing. 'Thanks.'

'Seems I'm outnumbered.' Ross sounded resigned.

Claire regarded him sceptically. He had given in far too easily for someone so much against this marriage. Committed to it now herself, regardless of the doubts still there, she wasn't going to let him put a spanner in the works whatever he might have in mind.

She got up to clear the plates, avoiding contact with Ross's long, lean fingers as he passed his across to her. His hands were well-kept; skin tanned a smooth golden brown, nails neatly trimmed. Capable of what, she didn't stop to consider.

'I'll bring the other dishes,' he offered unexpectedly. 'Save wheeling the trolley through.'

Claire would have preferred the trolley, but she wasn't being given the choice. Ross was already on his feet, gathering up both salad and potato bowls. He slanted a quizzical glance as she hesitated.

'Any problem with that?'

She shook her head, unable to frame a refusal. If he had any idea of talking her round to his point of view once they were alone, he could forget it. She had given her word. She couldn't and wouldn't go back on it now. What good would it do anyway? As Jill herself had said, they were both of them of an age to please themselves, and equally determined to do so.

Small as the kitchen was, Ross made it smaller still. He deposited the bowls on the work-surface where she indicated, but made no immediate attempt to return to the dining-room, leaning a hip against the cupboard to watch her transfer the apple pie from the pan in which it had been baked the previous evening on to a plate.

'You made that yourself,' he asked.

'Yes,' she said shortly. 'In the proper oven this time. Pastry doesn't come out too well in the microwave.'

'You must have found life very difficult being left with so much responsibility so young,' he observed. 'You said you had no other relatives?'

'There's a cousin on my mother's side in New Zealand, but he has a family of his own to take care of.' Claire kept her tone neutral. 'We've managed.'

'To keep your heads above water, maybe. I doubt if that business of yours brings in more than a bare living.'

'That depends on your idea of a bare living. *Our* needs are fairly simple.'

'How about desires?'

Claire swung to face him, the pie-slice clutched in her fist like a weapon. 'Are you by any chance suggesting that Jill might have deliberately set out to entrap a wealthy husband?'

She had taken off the jacket of her pale grey suit on coming home, but there had been no time to change. He took his time replying, his gaze moving down to the vulnerable hollow of her throat revealed by the open collar of her thin lemon-coloured blouse, and from there to linger for a moment on the swell of her small firm breasts, before lifting again to view her stormy face with an expression that made her feel inadequate in every sense.

'She wouldn't be the first,' he said hardily.

Claire calmed herself with an effort. Losing her temper was an indulgence which she couldn't afford right now. Not with this man.

'I see I was right in believing the capitulation a little too quick and easy,' she retorted. 'You're determined not to let it happen, aren't you?'

The grey eyes betrayed no discomfiture. 'I'm determined to safeguard Scott's future so far as I'm able, yes.'

'You only have to look at the two of them to see how much in love they are!' she declared.

His mouth twisted. 'You think that's all that's necessary for a marriage to work?'

'I think it's a good basis.'

'You're a romantic.' He made the words sound derogatory. 'What about when the passion wears off?'

Claire gave him back look for look. 'You're confusing love with lust.'

'I'm being realistic. Your sister is a very lovely girl. I can well understand how Scott could be carried away by her. Love of a kind, I'll grant you, but what do they really have in common?'

'What else is needed?' she asked, trying to convince herself. 'Jill might not have the same background, but she's hardly out of the gutter.'

'I wasn't suggesting either of you were that.' Ross was beginning to sound more than a little impatient. 'It isn't background I'm talking about.'

'Oh, I think it is. You just don't see Jill fitting in.'

There was a pause. He viewed her reflectively, hands thrust into trouser pockets in a manner far from relaxed. She was vibrantly conscious of his lean, fit length, of the latent strength in the broad shoulders and muscular forearms revealed by the pushed-up sleeves of his sweater. A man to be reckoned with in more ways than one; certainly not a man to make an enemy of. All the same, she had no intention of allowing him to walk roughshod over Jill's dreams.

'For someone who only learned of the situation a few hours ago, you've made a remarkably fast adjustment,' he observed. 'Maybe you see advantages for yourself too.'

Her eyes sparked, the pie-slice's handle digging into her palm as her fingers closed fiercely about it. She had a sudden urge to stick it between his ribs. When she did speak, her voice was low and husky.

'*I* neither want nor need *anything* from your family! All I care about is seeing Jill to rights. I'd have preferred a different start for her, obviously, but if your brother cares as much for her as she does for him—and I believe he does—then I'm ready to back them to the hilt.'

'Regardless of what it might do to my father?'

Claire had forgotten about that. It brought her up short for a moment.

'I realise it will be something of a shock for him,' she said at length, choosing her words with care, 'and I'm sorry it happened this way, believe me, but——'

'Not one half as sorry as I am,' came the grim interruption. 'I came here tonight hoping for some co-operation from you, but obviously I'm not going to get it.'

'Not the kind you're looking for, for certain,' she agreed. 'I think your brother is well able to make his own decisions.'

Ross straightened abruptly. 'You met him less than an hour ago. You've no idea what he's capable of. Jill isn't his first love.'

Claire stared at him, the wind knocked out of her. 'You're telling me he's been in this same situation before?'

'With regard to the pregnancy, no, but little more than a year ago he wanted to marry a girl he knew at Cambridge.'

She said tartly, 'Did he change his own mind, or did you manage to talk him out of it that time?'

'He realised what a fool he was being.'

'He's graduated now, and working for his living,' she pointed out. 'That surely makes a difference.'

'Older, but surely no wiser.' Ross was giving no quarter. 'He isn't even sure what he wants to do with his life as yet.'

'Yes, he is.' Claire was determined not to let the doubts take over. 'He wants to marry my sister.'

'And then what?'

'That's up to him to decide, isn't it? After all, he can hardly be destitute.'

'But you'd naturally have been just as ready to go along with this if he didn't have two pennies to rub together.'

The cynicism came across loud and clear. Not without some basis, Claire was bound to admit. She made a concentrated attempt to be totally honest about it.

'With a baby on the way, the financial aspect has to be important, of course. I'd hate to see Jill living hand to mouth. So, in that sense, the answer has to be no, I wouldn't have been as ready to go along.' She gave him no time to comment, her gaze unflinching. 'Not that I could have stopped her going ahead with the marriage regardless. At her age she's free to do whatever she thinks fit. The same way Scott is.'

Ross's lip curled a little. 'He's past the age of consent, certainly.'

'Then I'd suggest that you leave him to sort out his own affairs,' she said crisply. 'You can take the big brother theme too far.'

She turned away to pick up the plate containing the pie in one hand and the jug of cream in the other, feeling the shakiness in her lower limbs without surprise. There was something about Ross Laxton that would have rubbed her up the wrong way whatever the circumstances, she acknowledged. The fact that if Jill did marry Scott there would be other encounters was something she didn't want to think about.

He followed her back to the dining-room, taking his seat again without a word. Claire served the pie, trying hard not to let matters swamp her completely. This morning she had been worried that the weather would keep customers away again. It seemed such a ludicrously small concern now.

Scott was the first to break the silence. 'Whatever you tried on back there, you're not going to change anything,' he told his brother flatly. 'Jill and I are going to be married—and soon.'

'So you already said.' Ross's tone was level, his face expressionless. 'When do you plan on breaking the news?'

Scott hesitated, obviously a little thrown by the capitulation. 'When do you think might be the best time?'

'You're the one making the decisions.'

'In the morning, then.'

'Do you want me with you?' asked Jill.

The two brothers clashed glances, with the younger man's the first to fall.

'I think it might be best if I told them on my own,' he said.

'Of course.' She was obviously relieved. She added tentatively, 'I hope everything will be all right.'

'So,' said Ross meaningfully, 'do I.' He looked down at the untouched portion of pie on his plate, his mouth set. 'I'm afraid my appetite has deserted me.'

Claire was too het up to eat any more herself. She pushed away her own plate and got to her feet again. 'We'll have coffee in the sitting-room,' she said.

This time Ross made no offer of help. She had a feeling that if he hadn't driven Scott here to start with, he would have forgone coffee altogether. So far he had failed in his aim to call a halt to his brother's plans, but that didn't mean he would stop trying.

Whatever he might have in mind, he made no further reference. Scott offered no spoken demur when it was intimated that they would leave soon after the coffee had been drunk, although he was obviously reluctant to do so.

'I'll phone you as soon as I've got it over with,' he told Jill. 'They'll want to meet you. You too, of course,' he added to Claire. 'There'll be arrangements to make.'

'Let's take one step at a time,' suggested his brother. 'It's hardly as if the baby is due next week!' He gave Claire a brief nod. 'Thanks again for the hospitality.'

She inclined her head in return. 'You're welcome.'

Politeness so often involved telling lies, she reflected when the two of them had departed. They had been anything but welcome. The strain of the last few hours was beginning to tell on her. It was all she could do to keep a sense of proportion. There were worse things which could happen.

'So, what do you think of him?' asked Jill anxiously.

Does it matter what I think? Claire felt like asking, but managed a faint smile instead.

'He seems nice enough.'

'*Nice*?' Jill made it sound as if the word was an insult. 'He's just...wonderful!'

'You're the one in love with him, not me,' Claire pointed out. She hesitated before adding softly, 'I'd have thought the pair of you were sensible enough to at least take precautions.'

Her sister's colour rose, the expression in her eyes closer to guilt than defiance. 'You'd have thrown three fits if I'd gone on the pill!'

'I don't suppose I'd have known about it. In any case, it was as much Scott's place to take responsibility. More so, in fact, considering other risks.'

Jill gazed at her with knitted brows for a moment before the penny dropped. 'If you're talking about what I think you are, Scott's hardly in *that* category!' she declared indignantly.

'He doesn't have to be. You've seen all the warnings on TV.'

'They only apply to those who sleep around a lot. Scott isn't like that either!'

Claire wished she could be as certain. He didn't come across as the promiscuous type, but who could really tell these days? Jill almost certainly wasn't his first sexual experience; according to Ross, she wasn't even his first

love. Not that she had any intention of passing on that
piece of information.

She made a small wry gesture. 'I'm sure he isn't. But
neither is he blameless. From what Ross said, you were
still in school when this whole thing started.
Surely——'

'It wasn't Scott who made the running initially, it was
me.' Jill's chin was jutting, her mouth mutinous. 'I made
sure he noticed me that very first night.'

'In what way?'

'I asked him to dance.'

Claire felt her lips twitch involuntarily. 'That must
have taken a lot of courage,' she commented. 'What did
he say?'

'That he'd be delighted.' Jill's tone had softened into
reminiscence. 'He's so different from Rob, and Mark,
and the others. They'd make some stupid joke if a girl
asked any of *them* to dance.'

Claire could imagine. None of Jill's former boy-
friends was any older than she was herself, and certainly
no more mature. Scott's good looks were only a part of
the attraction. He had about him that same air of con-
fidence in himself that his brother possessed—although
he lacked the other's cutting edge.

'Do all your friends know you've been seeing Scott?'
she asked.

Jill shook her head. 'Just Lucy. I had to tell someone.'

Lucy was, and had been right since junior school, her
closest friend. The two of them told each other everything. Claire wondered just how capable the other girl
was of keeping mum when it came to news of this mag-
nitude. Everyone who could count would know the truth
soon enough once Jill began to show, of course, but by
that time she would be married, and not open to quite
the same degree of censure from those with nothing
better to think about.

Local opinion was hardly the main concern anyway. What mattered most was that Jill should be certain of what she was doing. Claire doubted if she had looked any further ahead than the immediate future.

'Do you think you'd have thought about marrying Scott if you hadn't got pregnant?' she said slowly, feeling for the words. 'I mean, *really* thought about it.'

The answer came swift and sure. 'Of course. He's everything I ever dreamed about!'

'I shouldn't have imagined you dreamt about marriage at all at your age,' Claire remarked mildly. 'I know I didn't.'

'I'm not you,' returned her sister with indisputable logic. 'I never wanted a career in the first place. You were always the ambitious one.'

And ambition was something which she had been forced to put aside to a great extent, Claire acknowledged ruefully. Sales was a long way from design, even if she did have her own business. She still kept her drawing-board set up in her bedroom, and occasionally worked on an idea, but time was too limited to consider it anything but a hobby.

'I wish you'd told me all this before,' she said, returning that particular dream to its niche. 'I honestly never realised how you felt about things.'

'It doesn't matter now, does it?' Jill obviously felt she could afford to be magnanimous. 'I've got what I want— or I shall have soon—and you'll be able to do whatever *you* want without worrying about me any more.'

That aspect hadn't occurred to her, Claire had to admit. Nor did she find it any consolation. She got up and went to draw the curtains, standing for a moment gazing out into the dusk. There was so much to be considered, so many details that Jill didn't appear to have got round to thinking about as yet.

'Have you discussed where you're going to live?' she queried, without turning.

'Not yet.' Jill sounded anything but concerned. 'We'll probably buy a house.'

Money might not be the main attraction in this relationship but it certainly had *some* bearing, Claire thought drily.

'Does Ross still live at the family home too?' she heard herself asking.

'No, he has a flat in town.'

Claire finished drawing the curtains and briefly contemplated regaining her seat, but she was too churned up inside to spend any more time going over and over the same ground.

'I think I'll make some cocoa,' she said. 'Do you want some?'

'No, thanks.' Jill was lying back in her chair, eyes closed, a far-away look on her face. 'I just want to think about Scott.'

Hair tousled, body still immature in the tight-fitting jeans and T-shirt, she looked nowhere near old enough to be having a baby. At that precise moment, Claire felt anything but benevolent towards the young man responsible.

CHAPTER THREE

UNUSUALLY for her, Jill was up and about by eight, impatient for the promised phone call. She would eat no more than a piece of toast for breakfast, and kept an eye constantly on the kitchen clock.

'Surely he must have told them by now!' she burst out when nine o'clock had come and gone. 'I mean, where's the point in waiting any longer?'

'I don't suppose his parents will be around all that early, considering his father's condition,' Claire suggested. 'Give him time. I'm sure he won't let you down.'

She mentally crossed her fingers as she said it, not at all certain that she was right. Ross had had a whole night to work on his brother. Who could tell what persuasions he might have employed?

With the sun shining outside for once, and the temperature more in keeping with the time of year, it should have been a morning for good cheer, but cheerful was the last thing she felt. Whatever happened, Jill's whole life was going to be so different from everything she had hoped for her. Eighteen was no age at which to be landed with a child, whatever the circumstances.

'I'm going out to mow the lawn,' she announced, unable to bear the inactivity. 'You could come and do a spot of weeding, if you like. You'll hear the phone ring if we leave the window open.'

Jill shook her head. 'I might not.'

Claire sighed and gave in. Obviously nothing was going to shift Jill far from the telephone until she had received the call. It was only to be hoped that it would come soon.

Wearing jeans and a cotton shirt, she went out and manhandled the ancient mower from the garden hut. It was almost ready to give up the ghost altogether, but with care it should just about see out this growing season. The modern hover mowers were so much easier, both to use and to maintain, by all accounts; next spring's budget would have to stretch to one.

Standing on his patio, contemplating his beautifully landscaped expanse of garden, their next-door neighbour lifted a hand in greeting as she wheeled the heavy machine into position for the first line of cut. The Johnsons were in their fifties, and had been very supportive during these past few years, but they had family of their own to care about. Their daughter, Susan, had been married a year, and was expecting her first baby in October. The way it should be, Claire reflected.

But that isn't the way it is, so stop carping and accept it, she told herself firmly. People could say what they liked, think what they liked. All that mattered in the end was that Jill was all right.

With the mower going, she didn't hear the phone ring. But Jill's emergence from the house, looking radiant with relief, was enough to confirm that the call had indeed come through.

'They want to meet me,' she declared. 'You too, Scott said. I told him we'd drive over this afternoon.' Her laugh was carefree. 'So much for all Ross's spouting on about what it would do to his father!'

Leaning on the mower, trying not to let her trepidation at the thought of facing the Laxtons *en masse* gain too much ground, Claire said carefully, 'It doesn't necessarily mean they're in total agreement with what's to be done.'

'Scott said they are.' She paused, her face clouding a little. 'At least, he didn't say they weren't.' Her expression firmed again. 'Anyway, they should be thankful we didn't just go off and get married without telling anyone at all.'

Claire considered her with drawn brows. 'You actually thought of doing that?'

'Well, it would have saved all this, wouldn't it? A *fait accompli* it's called.'

'I know what it's called.' Claire hardly knew whether to believe her or not. 'I'm glad you didn't.'

She looked at the stretch of lawn still to be cut, feeling anything but enthusiastic about completing the job. Only, if she didn't, who would? Jill had shown little interest in the garden at the best of times. In any case, should everything work out as planned, she wouldn't be here much longer.

It would seem strange to be on her own, Claire thought, depressed. Jill might not be much of a help around the house but she was someone to come home to in the evening, someone who made cooking a meal worthwhile. Life would be very empty without her.

She was running on ahead of herself again, she acknowledged at that point. Nothing was certain until it was an accomplished fact.

'You'd better start thinking about what you're going to wear this afternoon, if you want to create a good impression,' she said with forced lightness. 'There's that white dress you've never had on yet.'

Jill pulled a face, looking even younger than her years for a moment. 'I'm not dressing up like a dog's dinner just to create an impression,' she stated inelegantly. 'I'll wear what I feel comfortable in.'

What Jill felt comfortable in was either jeans or skirts more like wide belts, neither of which, Claire judged, would suit the Laxtons' sartorial tastes. On the other hand, what was the point in her trying to conform to a standard set by others? Scott had fallen for her the way she was, and his opinion was the important one.

'Fine,' she agreed. 'We both will. I'd better get on with this if I want to finish it before lunch. Heaven only knows when we'll have another dry day.'

'I'll get lunch ready, if you like,' offered Jill with a munificent air. 'You have enough to do.'

Considering that they were only having tinned salmon and last night's left-over salad, it would hardly take much effort, but Claire wasn't about to turn the offer down. 'That would be a big help,' she agreed.

If Jill registered any irony at all, she wasn't about to let it bother her. Hair swinging, hips slim as a boy's, she trotted off back to the house.

Watching her go, Claire felt a moment's near envy of her sister's buoyant spirit. So far as Jill was concerned, everything was going swimmingly. She wished that she could feel as confident of it herself.

Lunch over, the dishes washed and put away and a few other essential odd jobs taken care of, she went upstairs to take a shower and put on a crisp tan and white-striped cotton dress with short sleeves and a narrow-belted waist, sliding her feet into tan leather sandals with her favourite if not particularly fashionable three-inch heels.

Jill had topped her by the age of fifteen, and was now around five feet seven without the aid of shoes. Attempting to assert authority over someone several inches taller was no easy matter, Claire had long ago realised.

Not that it always followed. Her father had been a six-footer, her mother an inch shorter than Claire was herself, but her mother's word had been law. It was all down to strength of character, she supposed. When it came to any real battle of wills, Jill could beat her hands down any day of the week.

Which made an absolute mockery of Jill's claim to have been overruled when it came to choosing which universities to apply to for a place, she thought now, sitting down at the dressing-table to apply a light make-up. Jill had been only too vocal in stating where she wanted to go. That was before she had met Scott, of course. He had changed everything. It was only to be hoped that Claire's own first impressions of him proved sound in the long run.

The green eyes looking back at her from the mirror were less than convinced. No matter how much she tried to be optimistic, there was no guarantee that this marriage would last. Scott appeared OK on the surface, but who could tell what he was really like underneath? He might come to regret being tied down with a wife and child at such a comparatively early age, while his brother still enjoyed the freedom to pick and choose.

However, there was little she could do about it now, she acknowledged fatalistically. Marriage was a gamble whichever way it began.

Jill's choice of mid-thigh-length skirt and matching cropped jacket in pale blue was surprisingly demure. Her legs had lost the coltish look of a year or so ago and had gained a lovely shape. With her hair hanging straight and shining down to her shoulders, she was altogether a sight for sore eyes, thought Claire tenderly, though she was still so heart-breakingly young to be in this position.

Warmed by the sun after standing out on the drive, the Panda not only started first pull but sounded positively eager to be up and off. Which was more than she felt herself, Claire was bound to admit.

The Laxton home was out in Hope Valley, which meant going right through town. As anticipated on such a fine afternoon, the through-route was thronged with traffic heading for the Dales. Following a packed Ford Granada up a hill, she misjudged her gear-change on the steep bend, and received an irritated blast on the horn from the vehicle behind at her lack of acceleration.

'Road-hog!' shouted Jill as the car pulled out and roared past them, narrowly avoiding a head-on collision with one coming down the hill. 'Just because you're driving a blasted Porsche!'

'He can't possibly hear you,' Claire pointed out, and received a grin.

'I know, but it lets off steam. You should try it instead of just sitting there being all cool and collected.'

Only on the outside, reflected Claire wryly. The coming meeting promised to be anything but an easy-going affair. There would be awkwardness on both sides, with her own position, as Jill's guardian and supposed mentor, the most untenable of all. Who else could be held responsible for her young sister's seeming lack of moral values?

Hopefully, having shot his bolt last night, Ross would be absent. The last thing she needed was another confrontation with *that* individual.

They were three miles out of town amid open moorland when the front off-side tyre blew. Claire fought with the steering, which had gone suddenly extremely heavy, and brought the car to a jerky halt at the roadside.

'Damn!' she said forcefully. 'This would have to happen today of all days!'

'It's almost half-past three already,' announced Jill, as if it made any difference. 'What do we do now?'

Claire refrained from stating the obvious. Turning off the engine, she got out to go and open up the boot. She was hardly dressed for changing a wheel, but what choice did she have?

Next moment she was gazing disbelievingly at a spare tyre as flat as the proverbial pancake. Since she had had the last puncture repaired a couple of months back, it hadn't occurred to her to make a check. She'd simply taken it for granted that everything was OK.

Whatever had caused the leak, they were going to get no further on this than the one already on the car, she acknowledged ruefully. Which left them well and truly stranded.

'What's wrong?' asked Jill, getting out to see what was holding things up. She looked at the deflated tyre in dismay. 'Oh, no!'

'Oh, yes, I'm afraid.' Claire was apologetic. 'One of those classic situations you generally only see on film.'

'What do we do now?' Jill repeated. 'They'll think we're not coming!'

'Hardly.' Eyes on the fast-moving traffic, Claire tried to think. 'If Scott telephones the house he'll realise we've already left. He'll know something must have happened when we don't turn up inside another half an hour or so, and will probably come looking. In the meantime,' she added, with determined practicality, 'we'll just have to sit and wait.'

'We could thumb a lift,' suggested Jill hopefully 'There's sure to be somebody going that way.'

Claire shook her head. 'Hitching can be dangerous.'

'Not if it's a family.'

'If it's a family, there's unlikely to be room for anyone else. Anyway, it would be an imposition.'

Jill put on her most stubborn expression. 'Well, there's no harm in trying.'

She moved to the kerb, all hair and legs and winning smile as she lifted a hand in the time-honoured gesture. Two drivers tooted their horns but didn't stop, while the rest sailed past without acknowledgement.

Having pulled up just past a big bend, they were out of sight until it was too late for cars to signal a stop, Claire reckoned. A dangerous situation altogether, in fact. All it needed was for someone to take the bend too fast, and they'd be on them before they could pull out.

About to suggest that they push the car further along the road, she paused in consternation as the big silver Mercedes just flashing past signalled abruptly and pulled up some twenty yards or so ahead of them. Ross waited for a break in the following traffic before easing himself from behind the wheel to walk back to them.

Wearing a dark blue jacket and lighter blue trousers and shirt, he looked taller than ever—and certainly no less devastating. He took in the situation at a glance, face impassive.

'First thing is to get it further along the road so you don't cause an accident,' he said. 'You'd better get behind the wheel and make sure it doesn't veer out into the road while I push.'

'I can help,' offered Jill. 'I'm stronger than I look.'

It would have taken a heart of pure stone to resist the appeal in the wide hazel eyes, and Ross's, it seemed, wasn't totally hardened. His smile was reluctant but it was a smile, subtly altering the lines of his face.

'I can manage, thanks,' he said. 'I'd hate you to get that suit dirty.'

The Panda had been washed a couple of days ago, though the rain hadn't exactly kept it band-box clean, Claire had to admit. He would be lucky to get away without a mark on those pristine shirt-cuffs, to say the least.

She slid behind the wheel and released the handbrake, put the gear-shift into neutral and kept the car into the kerb as Ross pushed it steadily along. She could see the bent dark head and broad, blue-clad shoulders in the driving-mirror. Not formal dress, but not entirely casual either. Lunch with some woman-friend, perhaps?

No concern of hers whatsoever, she told herself. It was sheer bad luck that he had been passing at this particular time. He'd no doubt consider her a fool now, as well as a possible profit-seeker.

As she had expected, there were dusty streaks on the pale blue cuffs when he'd finished pushing. If he noted them himself, he showed no sign.

'Which road organisation are you with?' he asked. 'You can call them on the car-phone.'

'None,' Claire admitted, refusing to allow any hint of embarrassment to show in her voice.

Ross showed no visible reaction himself. 'It's unlikely that you're going to get anyone other than that out to see to it today,' he observed. 'You'll just have to risk leaving it here.'

'I have to be at the shop all day tomorrow,' said Claire concernedly, speaking her thoughts aloud.

Jill made a restless movement. 'You'll have to get a garage to fetch it in.'

That would cost a bomb, Claire knew, but there seemed little alternative. She would have to get to the shop by bus.

Ross dusted off his hands and nodded towards the Mercedes. 'Let's go.'

'I'm really sorry to put you to all this trouble,' she said, doing her best to sound genuinely apologetic. 'Especially if you were on your way somewhere.'

'I've been somewhere,' he returned. 'Lucky I decided to come back this way.' The grey eyes were derisive. 'Rescuing damsels in distress is my forte.'

'A real knight of the road!' she mocked back, giving way to the animosity which he aroused in her. 'You should choose a white steed next time.'

His glance rested a moment on her face, taking in the challenging tilt of her chin, the slight flush staining her high cheekbones; there was a glimmer of something approaching genuine humour in his eyes now. 'I'll bear it

in mind. In the meantime, you'll just have to settle for
common silver.'

Jill was already at the car, looking back impatiently
to where they still stood. 'It's going on a quarter to four!'
she called.

'As your sister so rightly points out, time is marching
on,' Ross observed. 'Shall we join her?'

Claire turned without another word and walked to the
car, nerves still quivering. Ross Laxton totally under-
mined what poise she possessed. He made her want to
hit out at him both verbally *and* physically.

Jill opened the rear door and slid inside as they approached, leaving Claire with little option but to take
the front passenger seat. Ross opened the door before
she could do it herself, inviting her in with a taunting
sweep of his hand.

'Your carriage awaits, ma'am. Don't forget to buckle
up.'

Sinking into the soft leather luxury, she reached for
the seatbelt, only to feel it snag on the ratchet as she
tried to pull it across. Ross slid into his seat, and leaned
across to take the belt buckle from her, easing it back
into the spool. She could feel the warmth of his breath
on her cheek, catch the faint scent of aftershave. The
blue-clad arm brushed her breast as he drew the belt out
again and clipped it home, sending a frisson down her
spine.

'You jerked it too hard,' he said. 'Inertia reels are sensitive to pressure.'

They weren't the only things, she thought, still feeling
the tingle. There was no denying her physical responses
where this man was concerned; he created mayhem with
her pulse-rate every time he came near. A purely instinctive reaction, and one she could do little about, unfortunately—except to make sure that he didn't guess
how he affected her.

'Thanks,' she said tersely.

He fired the ignition, a faint smile on his lips. Claire had a sudden feeling that he knew *exactly* how he affected her—the same way he probably affected every woman he came into contact with. Not that he'd find her particular response anything but amusing. His taste in women would run to the tall, blonde and sophisticated, if she was any judge at all.

The width of the car afforded plenty of room between the seats, but she still felt too close. His hand resting lightly on the gear-lever as he waited for a gap in the traffic was nowhere near her knee, yet she found herself shifting over to the left on the pretext of settling herself more comfortably in her seat, reluctant to allow even the slightest chance of any further contact.

'We're going to be awfully late,' said Jill from the rear, with a note of concern. 'Scott will think I'm not coming.'

'I doubt it.' Ross pulled out rapidly into the flow, accelerating smoothly away. 'He has the utmost faith in you.'

'No more than I have in him.' She was quiet for a moment before asking hesitantly, 'Were you there when he told your parents about us?'

'I was,' he confirmed. 'He needed moral support.'

'But you don't support him, do you?' Claire cut in. 'You made that clear enough last night.'

He glanced in the driving-mirror before signalling for the approaching junction, slowing down to take the right-hand turn with fine judgement. The road here was narrower, the low stone walls bounding it affording a panoramic view of the surrounding countryside, mellow in the afternoon sunlight.

'I can hardly claim to be over the moon about it all,' he returned, 'but I'm not about to turn my back on him because of it.'

'How did they take it?' queried Jill.

'How would you expect them to take it?' He sounded abrupt again. 'Oh, don't worry. They'll be civilised about it.'

'There's no point in being anything else, is there?' said Claire. 'What's done is done.'

'Well and truly,' he agreed with irony. 'All that's left is to make the best of a bad job.'

Jill was silent after that, but Claire could sense her simmering resentment. Ross wasn't making things any easier.

She kept a rein on her own tongue for the rest of the journey, saving herself for the coming encounter with his parents. Civilised they might be; acceptance was something else altogether. There was still a chance that, between the three of them, Scott could be persuaded to think again.

Big and square and covered in ivy, the Laxton house lay within beautifully maintained grounds. Even more imposing than she had anticipated, Claire acknowledged as Ross brought the car to a halt in the gravelled forecourt.

He got out and made as if to come round to the passenger side, shrugging when she disembarked herself and turning back to open the rear door for her sister, who accepted the courtesy as if accustomed to nothing else but.

Despite everything, Claire had to smile. Jill would have little difficulty in adapting to a new lifestyle. And it would be all of that. The Laxtons moved in a different world.

Scott came out from the house, his expression perturbed. 'What happened?' he asked.

'Tyre blow-out,' supplied his brother succinctly. 'Lucky I was passing.'

'The spare was flat, too,' Claire put in before he could make any further comment. 'It was supposed to have been repaired.'

Scott grinned. 'The same thing happened to me a couple of months back, only in my case I'd simply forgotten to get it done. Come on in.'

He ushered the two of them through to a hall panelled in rich dark oak. An archway to the rear framed an oak staircase, while another to the side of it gave access to what appeared to be an inner hall. A faded, though still lovely carpet covered much of the polished wooden floor.

The huge vase of gladioli set on a table between the two arches created instant warmth and colour. A friendly house, Claire found herself thinking; a family house with a lived-in atmosphere which she found heartening.

Ross opened a door on the left and stood back to allow the two of them prior access. Jill hung back, reaching for Scott's hand as if in search of Dutch courage, and giving Claire little choice but to go on ahead into the comfortably furnished sitting-room with its old stone fireplace filled with a further blaze of summer blooms.

Knowing about the stroke, it was still something of a shock to see Mr Laxton seated in a wheelchair. His face was gaunt, his left side obviously affected still, but there was nothing vague about the glance he turned her way, although he didn't attempt to speak. Claire felt somewhat at a loss for words herself.

Looking every inch the lady in her cream skirt and matching silk shirt, Mrs Laxton rose from her chair. Her expression was guarded, but there were signs of strain in the fine blue eyes.

'You're Jill?' she asked.

'No, this is Jill,' said her younger son from the rear. 'That's Claire.'

A handshake didn't seem suitable to the moment, thought Claire uncomfortably, and she was relieved when the older woman made no attempt to offer her hand.

'I think we'd all better sit down and have tea before we start talking things through,' she said. 'It will be here in a moment.'

As if on cue, there came a rattle of crockery from the hall, and the door which Ross had just closed opened again to admit a middle-aged woman wearing a dark blue dress and pushing a trolley.

'I set for six,' she announced, giving the two girls a frankly curious glance. 'The scones are freshly made, too.'

'Lovely,' said Mrs Laxton. 'Thank you, Alice.'

Claire took a seat on one of the two-seater sofas set at right angles to the fireplace as the woman departed, unsurprised when Jill and Scott elected to take the other together. She steeled herself not to react when Ross sat down at her side.

Both sons had inherited their father's colouring, although Mr Laxton's dark hair was mostly grey now. Their mother was fair, and a good-looking woman still. If she was right in taking Ross to be around thirty-three or four, Mrs Laxton would have to be in her fifties, Claire judged, yet she could probably have passed for forty-five.

Mr Laxton was able to handle his cup all right, she was relieved to see. So far, he hadn't said a word. She wondered if the paralysis affected his speech.

The situation was worsening by the minute, she thought unhappily. She could understand why Ross had been so concerned for his father's welfare. The man was in no fit state to be dealing with the kind of stress which Scott and Jill between them had forced on him.

'Scott tells me you lost your parents several years ago,' said Mrs Laxton. 'That must have been terrible for you.'

'It took a lot of getting over,' Claire acknowledged, doing her best to keep an even tone.

'As much as you can ever get over something like that.' The sympathy was obviously genuine. Mrs Laxton's gaze shifted to Jill, who had been unusually silent up to now. 'I blame Scott for this, not you, dear. You're so young!'

'It's just as much my fault,' Jill declared loyally, and with some truth.

'Apportioning blame isn't going to alter anything,' put in Ross, on an acrid note. 'The question is, what's to be done about it?'

'That's already been decided,' said Scott shortly. 'We're going to be married.'

'That goes without saying, of course,' agreed his mother. 'And without too much delay. What we need to discuss is where and when?'

'St James's.' Spoken in slightly slurred tones, the statement drew all eyes to the man seated in the wheelchair.

His wife hesitated. 'Wouldn't it be better to use the Register Office?'

'No.' Slurred or not, the tone was adamant. 'I'll have no son of mine married in a Register Office!'

'I don't mind being married in church,' said Jill into the pause. 'Although I don't suppose I should really wear white.'

'Plenty of others do,' declared her husband-to-be. To his father, he added, 'Is it such a good idea though, Dad? The Register Office would be quieter.'

'It's unlikely that St James's will be able to fit it in this side of autumn, anyway,' Ross pointed out. 'Summer is a popular time for weddings.'

'They're only busy on Saturdays,' declared his father stubbornly, struggling to get the words out.

'It can still be a quiet wedding, even in church,' said Claire, colouring a little as all eyes turned her way. 'I mean,' she tagged on quickly, 'it doesn't have to be full choral and all that, does it?'

It was Ross who answered. 'If you're worried about the cost, it will hardly be your concern.'

Her head came round with a jerk, eyes darkening angrily as she met his gaze. 'It most certainly will!'

'Can you afford to finance a wedding?' he asked. 'Even a small one is likely to cost a fair sum, and business hasn't been so good this year, I imagine.'

He would probably have had a check run on her by now, Claire reckoned. There were ways and means even at the weekend.

Under the terms of her agreement, the renewal of her lease was dependent on the projected future of the business at the time; low profits hardly guaranteed regular payment of dues. The shop occupied a prime location. Even in today's financial climate there would very likely be no shortage of takers should the lease come on the market again. It was another concern to be taken on board.

The money invested for Jill's further education wouldn't be needed now, of course. That might provide enough of a buffer to get her through the season. On the other hand, there was no way that she was going to allow the Laxtons to pay for everything, she thought staunchly.

'Things will pick up again now the weather's turned,' she claimed, hoping that today wasn't just a one-off. 'In any case, we do have other income.'

Jill opened her mouth to say something, caught Claire's eye, and shut it again, although her face reflected the doubt she had almost expressed. Ross viewed her thoughtfully before turning his attention back to Claire.

'There are times,' he said almost conversationally, 'when pride is misplaced.'

Oblivious for the moment of the others in the room, Claire held the penetrating gaze, seeing sudden tawny lights flicker to life in the grey depths. She felt her stomach muscles contract, her skin prickle as if ants were crawling all over her. It took everything she had to keep from betraying the effect he had on her in her voice.

'Not this time.'

CHAPTER FOUR

TEN minutes later it was settled: the wedding at St James's at a date to be arranged, providing it was no more than a month or so from now.

According to her own calculations, Jill would only be around eight or nine weeks gone by then, and unlikely to be showing any sign. Not that that was by any means the most important factor to be taken into consideration, in Claire's view.

Scott was to take his wife-to-be into Sheffield the following afternoon to visit a gynaecologist with whom he had, it appeared, already made an appointment. Claire still held on to the faint hope that it would all turn out to be a mistake. Girls of Jill's age often went through hormonal irregularities.

Whether Scott would still be as ready to marry her should that happen was another matter, though his feelings for her seemed to be genuine enough on the face of it. Jill would be devastated if it all fell through; first love was so intense.

And what would she know about it? she asked herself wryly at that point. There had been one or two men in her life during the past few years, but none for whom she had come close to feeling anything in depth. The one whom she was seeing on a fairly regular basis at present was away on holiday in Scotland until Tuesday. He had wanted her to go with him, but she hadn't been able to afford to pay someone else to look after the shop, even if there had been anyone she could have trusted to do so.

In any case, while Andrew was fine to spend the odd evening with, they really didn't have all that much in common. He was very much into organised sport, which she found boring for the most part. She had already more than half decided to let the whole thing peter out when he got back.

'You're looking very introspective,' Ross remarked, jerking her out of her reverie. He was watching her closely, an odd expression in his eyes.

'There's a lot to think about.' She turned her attention away from him to look across at his mother. 'What about the reception?'

'We can hold that here,' the older woman declared. 'If it's to be just family and close friends, we don't need to bother with a marquee.' Her smile was still far from spontaneous. 'There's always the terrace if it turns out to be a nice day.'

Jill and Scott were the only ones likely to have that, Claire reflected. For the rest of them it would simply be a day to get through. A shotgun wedding Ross had called it—though that surely only applied when the groom was an unwilling participant. Whatever, it wasn't an occasion to be exactly joyful about.

All she wanted to do at the moment was to go home. Jill, however, looked anything but ready to leave. She and Scott were talking quietly together, heads bent close, eyes locked. They made an attractive couple, Claire had to admit. If only things could have been different!

'Nothing's been said about where the two of you are going to live,' she mentioned, thinking it was time someone did.

'There's plenty of room here,' answered Mrs Laxton before either could speak. 'The room next to Scott's used to be the nursery. It will make a fine one again, with a little refitting.'

'Oh, good.' Scott sounded as if he hadn't given the matter a great deal of thought. 'That will be great, won't it, Jill?'

'Great,' she echoed, not sounding quite so sure.

Claire could hardly blame her. Young married couples usually moved in with parents only when money was so tight that they could afford to do nothing else—and even then only for the time it took them to raise the where-withal to get their own place. Quite apart from anything else, Mr Laxton himself was in no fit state to be disturbed by a crying baby.

All the same, it wasn't really her place to raise any objection, she acknowledged, although she had to bite her tongue to stop herself. Jill would have to have a word with Scott in private.

Catching Ross's eye, she gathered the impression that he had a very good idea of what she was thinking, and that this was one factor on which they were in agreement. Not that it was up to him either.

'Scott tells me you're interested in gardening,' he said unexpectedly. 'Perhaps you'd like to have a look round the grounds while you're here?'

He wanted her removed before she could upset the apple cart even further, Claire surmised. Reluctant though she was to accept the invitation, she could find no adequate reason to refuse.

'That's very... kind of you,' she murmured.

Judging by the faint slant of his lip, her hesitation over the choice of word had not gone un-noted. 'Isn't it, though? We'll have to stick to the paths, of course. Those heels of yours aren't made for softer ground.'

'Oh, I don't know.' She kept her tone light, her expression guileless. 'I use them to aerate the lawns at home.'

Mr Laxton chuckled, drawing all eyes to him. Impeded by the paralysis pulling down one corner of his mouth, his smile was more of a grimace.

'Biter bit!' he got out.

Ross's grin was unexpected. 'Nipped, at any rate.' He rose lithely to his feet, looking down at Claire from what seemed like a long distance. 'Let's get to it, then.'

She got up slowly, vitally aware of the disparity both in height and sheer self-possession. Right now she would have given her eye-teeth for a little more of both. Ross might have been forced to accept the situation but that didn't mean he had to like it, any more than it meant he had to like either her *or* Jill. She had a feeling that he would be making that more than clear.

The sun was still out, its warmth very welcome after the unseasonal coolness of the past few weeks. Below the wide stone-balustraded terrace at the rear of the house flowerbeds interlaced with gravelled paths, which stretched down through a rose-covered pergola to tree-shaded lawns, where neither moss nor mole-hills marred the emerald perfection.

Almost too chocolate-box perfect, in fact, Claire reflected, then took herself to task for allowing envy to warp her judgement.

Ross had made no attempt to start a conversation since leaving the house, but just strolled along at her side, hands thrust into trouser pockets. He made her feel inadequate just by being there.

'It must have been wonderful growing up here,' she commented at length, unable to think of anything more riveting to say. 'Always providing you did, of course?'

'I did,' he returned. 'Not that I was around all that much.'

'Boarding-school?' she hazarded, and received a glance.

'You don't approve of children being sent away to school?'

'No, I don't,' she said firmly. 'A child's place is with its parents.'

'Depends on the child. Personally, I wouldn't have missed the experience.'

'I'm sure *you* found it ideal.'

Dark brows lifted a fraction. 'You're suggesting that I might have lacked sensitivity as a child?'

The mockery in his tone put an extra spur to the antipathy he aroused in her. 'Why stop at the child?' she asked with acid inflexion. 'You're about as sensitive as an alley-cat now!'

He laughed, shaking his head admiringly. 'I bet you're a little hellion when you really let go!'

It was the 'little' that did it. Without stopping to think about it, she spun round and hit him viciously across one lean cheek, aware of a momentary surge of satisfaction as she saw his expression undergo an abrupt change and heard the sharp expletive jerked from his lips. Horror followed almost immediately as she realised what she had just done. Face flaming, she took an involuntary step backwards, away from him.

Ross regarded her in withering disgust. 'How old did you say you were?'

About to stammer an apology, Claire was overtaken by another irrepressible surge of white-hot anger. 'Old enough not to take ridicule lying down!' she snapped.

The grey eyes acquired a dangerous glint. 'Then let's play it the adult way.'

His hands, fastening about her upper arms to jerk her up to him, were like steel bands, his mouth a trap, crushing any protest she might have made. Too stunned to struggle, Claire was conscious of conflicting emotions as the hardness of his lips gave way to something infinitely more disturbing. When he finally let her go she was hot and flushed and speechless.

'Hit me again and I might feel moved to return an eye for an eye,' he declared.

Lips burning, stomach muscles tense as bow-strings, she looked at him with loathing. 'Nothing you did would surprise me,' she jerked out. 'You really think you're *it*, don't you?'

'That depends,' he returned drily, 'on what "*it*" is exactly.'

'In your case, lord of the whole damned manor!'

His sudden grin was a goad in itself. 'You certainly live up to that hair of yours, don't you? I only hope none of your customers ever get across you!'

'I treat,' she said tautly, 'the way I find. My customers aren't boors!' She drew in a steadying breath. 'For the record, I don't like the situation any more than you do, but unlike you I recognise your brother's right to run his own life. Your parents seem to have come to terms with it all pretty well.'

The amusement faded. 'On the surface, perhaps. They've had more than their fair share of stress these last few months. Lord only knows what this is doing to them underneath.'

Claire caught her lower lip between her teeth. 'I'm sorry,' she said. 'That was insensitive of me.'

'Seems we might have something in common after all.' His expression dispassionate again, he lifted his shoulders in a brief, dismissive shrug. 'We may as well go back to the house.'

Claire followed slowly in his wake as he turned back the way they had come. Hitting him had been a mistake in more ways than one, she acknowledged ruefully. Not only had she shown herself up, she had given him the opportunity to cut her down to size in a way that had left too lasting an impression for comfort.

Nothing had been altered by it all, either. For better or for worse, Jill and Scott were going to be married. Hopefully, it would veer towards the better rather than the worse, but there were no guarantees. Even the most seemingly well-suited couples could run into difficulties.

Mr Laxton was missing when they got back to the sitting-room. He needed a rest before dinner, his wife explained.

'This hasn't been easy for him,' she added. 'He always anticipated that Ross would marry first. We both did.'

'I'll tie that particular knot when *I'm* good and ready,' growled Ross softly, causing Claire to suspect an on-going argument.

She glanced surreptitiously at her watch, surprised to find that it was still barely five-fifteen. Jill showed little inclination to leave, but they could hardly stay on for the rest of the day.

'I think it's time we were going,' she said, trying to sound positive about it. 'We seem to have everything sorted out.'

'Down to the last brass tack,' agreed Ross with satire. 'I'm going back to town myself. I'll drop the two of you off.'

'I'll take them,' declared his brother. 'We can have another look at that tyre on the way.'

'It really is too flat to be any use,' Claire assured him.

'Could be a very slow leak, in which case we could pump in enough air to get you home. I'll take the electric pump along anyway, and try it. Better if we don't have to leave it stuck at the roadside all night.'

Claire could only agree with that point of view. There was every chance, too, that Scott could be right, and that the leak would be slow enough to hold for at least the length of time it would take to drive home.

'Thanks,' she said gratefully. 'My foot-pump would take far too long.'

'I'll contact the vicar first thing in the morning and try to arrange a date,' promised Mrs Laxton, evidently not too loath to have them depart. 'You'll be back for dinner, Scott?'

Claire took the slight hesitation before he answered as reluctance to commit himself. 'You're welcome to eat at our place again,' she offered impulsively.

'I thought I might take the two of you out to dinner instead,' he said. 'We could make it a foursome if you're not already fixed up,' he added to his brother. 'The Padstock will find us a table.'

'Why don't you and Jill go on your own?' suggested Claire hastily, not caring to view the older man's expression. 'I've several things to catch up on, anyway.'

'Nothing that can't be left for another day, I'm sure.' It was impossible to tell from Ross's tone what his true reaction might be. 'You provided dinner last night, now it's our turn. I'll give the Padstock a ring.'

Claire controlled herself with an effort as he went from the room. The last thing she wanted was to spend another evening in Ross Laxton's company. It was surely the last thing he would have wanted himself. All he'd had to do was claim a previous engagement.

It was odd that he didn't appear to have one anyway, she thought. She didn't see him spending many evenings alone.

Jill looked happy enough at the proposal. The worst was obviously over so far as she was concerned. Whether she would object to Scott's ready acceptance of his mother's suggestion that they live here, Claire couldn't be sure. It might well have been that she'd seen advantages in a home where meals continued to be prepared and housework was done without a finger lifted on her part, especially with a baby on the way. All the same, it would be far from ideal.

Ross returned to confirm a reservation for eight-thirty at the up-market hotel reputed to run one of the finest restaurants in the county. Claire had been there once with Andrew, who had almost collapsed at the size of the bill. It had been his idea to go there in the first place, but he hadn't resisted when she had insisted on paying her share. She preferred going Dutch on most occasions anyway.

Tonight would hardly be one of those occasions. The Laxtons could no doubt well afford to eat at such places. The Padstock lay closer to here than home, which meant a lot of travelling for whoever elected to fetch and return. Even if Scott managed to inflate the tyre sufficiently to exchange it, she wouldn't dare risk using the Panda again until both tyres had been given a clean bill of health.

Scott's car was a low-slung sports job with a rear seat scarcely adequate to take an adult of even Claire's slender build. She did her best to stop her knees from digging into the back of the driving-seat as they set off at an acceleration that had the tyres spinning on the gravel. Cramped though it might have been, it was still infinitely preferable to driving back with Ross at the wheel.

The car was where they had left it. Scott drew in a few feet ahead, and took the pump along to connect it to the Panda's cigarette lighter.

'It will take about fifteen minutes to inflate,' he said, when he had the spare tyre out on the kerb and the pump running smoothly. 'Always providing it doesn't run out as fast as we're putting it in, of course,' he added cheerfully.

Much to Claire's relief, it didn't appear to be doing that. Fully inflated, the tyre looked as good as new—or as close to new as it had been in the first place. Looking at the tread, she doubted if it was even legal any longer, although it would have to do for now. Fortunately, tyres of this size didn't cost a bomb.

Scott insisted on following them all the way back to the house just in case. Jill elected to drive with him rather than accompany Claire. She could see the pair of them whenever she glanced in the driving-mirror, laughing and chatting almost non-stop.

Scott was one of those drivers who had to turn his head towards the person he was addressing, taking his eyes off the road for seconds at a time: a dangerous habit even at the relatively low speed they were doing now. If she had to jam on her brakes for any reason during those seconds of inattention, he could easily pile into her.

They arrived at the house without incident, but the concern remained. If he normally drove at the speed he had sustained on the initial part of the journey, that habit of his could get the pair of them killed. What to do about it was something else.

'Ross will pick you up around seven-thirty,' Scott advised. 'I'm not going to have time to get home, change, and come all the way back again myself.' He gunned the engine for a fast take-off, lifting a hand in smiling farewell.

A charmer on the surface but irresponsible in more ways than one, Claire reflected. His feelings for Jill might be genuine enough, but self-interest would take precedence. He certainly hadn't been too concerned about upsetting his father.

'Isn't he just fabulous!' Jill enthused, watching the car speed away. 'I must ring Lucy and tell her the news.'

'We only have an hour or so before Ross is due,' Claire reminded her, only too well aware of the length to which such a conversation could stretch. 'You can tell Lucy all about it tomorrow.'

For once Jill gave in without argument. 'I suppose you're right. We don't have a lot of time. I haven't even decided what to wear yet.'

Neither, thought Claire, had she. Nor could she summon any enthusiasm for the task. Ross Laxton was hardly worth taking any trouble over.

All the same, she found herself fingering through just about every item in her wardrobe before finally settling on a lightweight suit which she had designed and made up herself in a linen-mix fabric of muted greens and creams. The skirt just skimmed her knees, and the braided jacket hugged her waist. Under it she wore a plain green top in the same linen-mix, with her only jewellery a simple gold necklet and matching earrings.

Viewing herself in the long wardrobe mirror, she felt far from satisfied, but refused to change again. It was bad enough being dragged out on this dinner-date at all, without worrying about how she looked. Ross was the last man likely to be impressed by her appearance, whatever she wore.

Jill looked youthfully radiant in a simple off-white shift that left her long, smoothly tanned legs bare from mid-thigh. In a few weeks that flat stomach would be no more, thought Claire despondently. Jill burgeoning with child was hard enough to imagine—Jill as a mother even more so.

The Mercedes drew up as the hall clock struck the half-hour. Claire would have expected no less. She gave Ross no time to come knocking on the door.

Standing by the car, he appraised the two of them openly as they came towards him. He was wearing silver-grey trousers and a darker grey checked jacket himself, his shirt snowy beneath. He looked, Claire was bound to acknowledge, overwhelmingly attractive.

'Right on time,' he commented, opening both front and rear passenger doors. 'Quite a bonus.'

This time Claire gave Jill no opportunity to take the rear seat, sliding in quickly. 'Your turn to sit up front,' she directed as her sister hesitated.

Ross showed no reaction. Claire doubted if he could care less *who* sat up front. He was here only because his brother had made refusal awkward. They were in the same boat so far as that was concerned. Not that it made her feel any better inclined towards him.

Never one to remain silent for long, Jill loosened up after a few minutes and started chatting as if she had known Ross for years. He responded easily enough, laughing at some of her observations, but Claire still sensed that element of withdrawal.

From where she sat, she could see his eyes when he lifted them to the driving-mirror, and found it almost impossible to avoid clashing glances from time to time.

Detest him though she might, there was no getting away from his masculine charisma. The crisp line of dark hair at his nape, the powerful breadth of his shoulders, the faint, elusive scent of his aftershave all combined to create havoc with her senses. Chemistry, nothing more, but powerful all the same. She wished it were possible to find a neutralising formula.

He drove straight to the hotel. Scott was waiting for them in the bar. He stood up on their approach, tall, slim and somewhat overwhelmed by the unstructured lines of his casual suit—the kind of male fashion that Jill found spot-on but which did nothing at all for her, Claire had to admit. She preferred clothes that looked as if they had been made for the person wearing them.

With the two younger members of the party totally absorbed in each other, she and Ross had little choice but to talk to each other. He was far more at ease than she was, keeping something of a conversation going even when she responded in monosyllables.

The meal was superb, though Claire felt that she failed to do justice to it. She drank sparingly of the excellent wine, and refused a brandy with her coffee on the grounds that it tended to give her insomnia. Keeping a clear head seemed essential tonight.

They had eaten out on the terrace in the warm evening air, and watched a glorious sunset. In other company Claire would have relished every moment. As it was, she could hardly wait for the evening to end.

Toying with her coffee-spoon, listening with half an ear to Jill's and Scott's murmuring voices, she considered various excuses for calling a halt to the proceedings. It was still too early for a plea of tiredness to hold any water. Not that she imagined Ross for one would be loath to accept it, but Jill would almost certainly question the validity of any such claim.

'We're going for a stroll,' announced Scott, jerking her out of her thoughts. 'We shan't be long.'

'Mind how you go in the dark,' advised his brother. 'We don't want any accidents.'

Jill laughed. 'Don't worry, I eat lots of carrots.' She waved an airy hand, the other clasped close by Scott. 'See you in a little while.'

Claire watched the pair of them drop down the short flight of stone steps and disappear into the dimly lit gardens. She couldn't bring herself to look at the man seated opposite—couldn't think of a single word to say.

It was Ross who finally spoke, his tone dry. 'Congratulations on making such an effort.'

'I'm not the only one coerced into being here,' she retorted. 'You should have refused while you had the chance.'

'And forgo the opportunity to try forging a better relationship?'

Her head came up sharply, eyes sparkling in the candlelight. 'You're no more interested in a better relationship than a spider is with a fly! If you could find a way of stopping Scott from marrying Jill, you'd seize the opportunity with both hands. Don't think I don't know it!'

'You're quite right, I would.' He was angry himself, but holding it well in check, the only sign being a tensing of muscle along the lean jaw-line. 'They're neither of them in any way mature enough to take on the responsibility.'

'Couples younger than they are have managed to make a go of it.'

He made an impatient movement. 'I'm not just talking about years. Right now they're besotted with one another, but how long will it last?'

It was the same question Claire had asked herself, and she was no nearer an answer. She was not, however, prepared to give him the satisfaction of hearing her express the same doubts.

'As long as cynics like you stop trying to put a damper on it, it might last a lot longer than you think,' she retorted. 'Just because you've never felt that way about anyone yourself——'

She broke off abruptly, flushing a little as he tilted a sardonic lip.

'Maybe you're into palm-reading too?'

'I withdraw the remark,' she said tautly. 'It was presumptuous.'

'Yes, it was. True enough up to a point, however. I prefer to keep my feet firmly on the ground.'

'How very limiting!'

His mouth quirked, the grey eyes acquiring a sudden gleam of humour. 'Metaphorically speaking, that is.' He added smoothly, 'How about your own love-life?'

'That,' she said, 'is *my* affair!'

Too late she caught the ambiguity of the statement. Ross's grin drew a reluctant smile of her own.

'My own business, at any rate,' she amended. 'Anyway, it's neither you nor me we're here to discuss.'

'I'd say we already reached impasse where the other matter's concerned, so we may as well shelve it,' he said decisively. 'If we're going to be family, I suppose we'd better start trying to get along.'

Claire eyed him suspiciously, not at all sure that he really meant it. Minus their former hard derision, the grey eyes returned a level regard.

'Pax?' he queried.

'Pax,' she confirmed after a moment, and felt a cautious relief. Better not to have this man as an out-and-out enemy—particularly in light of their business connection. She would have a problem finding other premises as well-placed.

CHAPTER FIVE

'SO WHAT else *do* you do with your life apart from work?' Ross continued. 'Not that a six-day week can leave you with a great deal of spare time.'

'Five and a half,' Claire corrected. 'I close at one on Thursdays.' She gave a shrug. 'The usual things, I suppose. I like to get out walking when I can. My father was a keen rambler; he took me with him from quite an early age.'

'Not Jill too?'

'Jill takes after my mother on that score. She could never see the attraction in walking miles just for the sake of it, either.'

'Up hill and down dale.' Ross both sounded and looked totally relaxed for the first time that evening. 'I'm something of a rambler myself.'

'You are?' She couldn't hide the scepticism.

His smile was easy. 'Why the surprise?'

'You just don't seem the type,' was all she could come up with.

'You mean I look too weak and wan for a fresh-air fiend?'

Considering the lean, tanned features, the broad shoulders, the depth of chest revealed by his opened jacket, Claire had to smile herself. 'I was thinking more of the kind of lifestyle someone in your position would be likely to lead. Running a company like HR must be a full-time job in itself.'

'It can be,' he agreed. 'But there's such a thing as delegation. I've no intention of devoting my entire life to the company the way my father did. He might not be sitting there in a wheelchair if he'd allowed himself a little more leisure time.' He rolled the brandy balloon slowly between his hands, his expression suddenly austere. 'It took a stroke to make him see sense.'

His shirt-cuffs had pulled back enough to reveal a wafer-thin gold watch spanning a supple wrist lightly coated in dark hair. Her voice sounded husky to her ears. 'At least he's still alive.'

Ross looked up, the austerity fading. 'You must miss your parents a great deal.'

'All the time,' she admitted. 'I've learned to live with it, but the first year was dreadful. For Jill too, of course.'

'Except that she wasn't landed with the liability of looking after a fourteen-year-old.'

She said softly, 'According to what you told me yesterday, I haven't made too good a job of it.'

The shrug was brief. 'You could say she turned out no worse than Scott. All we can hope for now is a quick metamorphosis into responsible adulthood for the two of them.'

'Not to detract in any way from your mother's generosity, but they really need to be on their own,' Claire submitted, after a slight hesitation. 'Your father needs peace and quiet too.'

Ross studied her thoughtfully for a moment before answering. 'The house is big enough, but I take your point. I'll talk to Scott.'

A waiter arrived with the bill. Looking around, Claire realised that they were the last diners left on the terrace, although music was still being played inside. Of Jill and Scott there was no sign.

'Just how big are the grounds here?' she asked as the waiter departed with the gold card Ross had given him. 'They couldn't get lost in the dark, could they?'

'I doubt if they've gone far,' he said. 'Love's young dream craves privacy, that's all. We were cramping their style.'

'Perhaps we should go and find them,' she ventured. 'I mean, they obviously want us to leave the table.'

Ross shrugged. 'We leave the table when we're ready. Still, if you're eager to go...'

'I have to be up earlier than usual in order to take the Panda to the garage before I go to the shop,' Claire explained a little lamely, unwilling to admit to any reluctance to have the evening end.

'That tyre will most likely be flat again by morning,' he pointed out.

'I can always pump it up again.'

'Better still,' he said after a slight pause, 'why don't I come and pick you up? Let the garage fetch the car in.'

'I couldn't put you to all that trouble,' she objected swiftly. 'In any case, it would cost far too much to have the garage come out.'

'All right, so we'll drop both tyres off on the way and pick them up at the end of the day. And before you say it,' he added as she opened her mouth to protest further, 'I'm as capable as Scott of changing a wheel.'

'I don't doubt it.' Claire looked at him uncertainly. 'It really isn't necessary. If the worst comes to the worst, I can always take the bus.'

'And still have the same problem facing you. From what I saw of them, you could probably do with replacement tyres all round. They looked pretty close to the limit.'

Claire did a quick mental calculation of what five new tyres were likely to cost, and felt her heart sink. There were so many other bills due this month; this was one she could well have done without. Ross was right, though, safety came first. There was also the risk of having some gimlet-eyed policeman spot the worn tread.

'Which makes it even more necessary to take the whole car in,' she said, reconciling herself to the inevitable. 'Not that I'm not grateful for the offer,' she added hastily, 'but I'll manage—really.'

Ross gave a brief nod. 'Have it your own way.'

It was difficult to tell whether he was annoyed or not. Claire suspected that the gesture had been made more in the name of common courtesy than from any real personal interest in her welfare. They might not be enemies any more, but they were far from being friends.

She was relieved to see Jill and Scott coming back up the steps. Jill's eyes were starry, her hair tangled, as if fingers had been run through it. When she turned she displayed a large grass-stain on the back of her dress.

Claire saw Ross note it too, and draw the same conclusion, if his expression was anything to go by. Not that it made any difference now what the two of them got up to, she supposed, but this was hardly the place.

The waiter returned with the docket for signature. With that transaction completed, and the party reunited, there was no further reason to linger.

'I'll do the return journey,' declared Scott on the hotel steps.

'Hardly ideal for the rear-seat passenger,' his brother observed. 'Particularly as I'm going in the same direction.'

'So you take Claire,' the younger man suggested.

He gave neither of them time to utter a protest, seizing Jill by the arm and running her towards the car park, both of them laughing as if at some shared joke.

'Seems we're on our own,' commented Ross drily.

'I'd have been fine in the back of Scott's car.' Claire scarcely knew what else to say.

'Except that you quite obviously weren't wanted. It's no problem so far as I'm concerned,' he added. 'As I said, I'm going that way in any case.'

There was no point in any further discussion, Claire conceded. If she was any judge at all, the other two had planned for this to happen. Jill was for it when she saw her again, she thought wrathfully.

The Lotus roared past them as they walked to the car. Scott sounded a loud blast on the horn in total disregard of the by-laws, while Jill waved cheekily. They were both grinning like Cheshire cats.

'Like a pair of schoolkids!' Ross remarked.

Claire could only agree. Scott's twenty-two years sat very lightly.

Seated once more in the Mercedes, she found it hard to believe that it wasn't all that much more than twenty-four hours since Ross had come to the shop. She felt she had lived half a lifetime between times.

She stole a glance at him as he turned the car out into the road, experiencing the tensing of muscle and sinew that was fast becoming familiar as she appraised the clean-cut profile. His physical attraction was undeniable—though she didn't know what good acknowledging it was likely to do her. Apart from the stated hiking interest—which she still tended to regard as just so much talk—they were like chalk and cheese.

'Comfortable?' he asked, without taking his eyes from the road.

She gave a laugh. 'It would be difficult to be anything else in this!'

'As good an advertisement as any.' He added casually, 'You'd find the 190 a good second-hand buy, and not too expensive to run.'

'I'm happy enough with the Panda.' Claire had no intention of considering another car of any make, much less a Mercedes! 'Apart from a couple of punctures, and an oil leak, it's never let me down. That big snowfall this last winter—I was one of the few who didn't get stuck.'

'That could be down to the driver as much as the car.'

'According to most men, women don't make good drivers in *any* conditions.'

'Depends on the woman.'

She wasn't by any means faultless, Claire could have told him. There had been one or two occasions recently when she had come close to trouble through not keeping her attention wholly on the road. This new development had temporarily ousted her financial problems from the forefront of her mind, but they still existed. If trade didn't pick up over the next few weeks, she was going to find herself in a very difficult position all round.

What she certainly wouldn't be doing was appealing to Ross for any leeway where the lease's renewal was concerned, she told herself emphatically. She could imagine the interpretation he would put on that!

'You've gone quiet again,' he commented, after some moments had passed. 'There's no point dwelling on things. We just have to hope for the best where those two are concerned.'

'I know. And I'm sure they'll be all right.' Claire did her best to sound optimistic. 'Especially if they can be on their own.'

'I already said I'd have a word with Scott.' There was a slight edge to his voice. 'I can't do any more.'

'I realise that. It's Scott who would be financing a place of their own, so it has to be his decision, of course. I just...'

She let the rest peter out, aware of having said too much already. Jill wouldn't thank her for interfering if it caused any trouble between her and Scott. He had certainly seemed happy enough to accept his mother's offer.

'Do you have a busy day ahead of you tomorrow?' she asked, more from a need to change the subject than through any real desire to know.

'Board meeting,' came the succinct reply. 'If it follows the usual pattern, we'll be arguing the toss all morning.'

'As chairman, can't you put your foot down?' she suggested, tongue-in-cheek, and was relieved to see him smile again.

'It would do more good lofted upwards in some departments. I'm fighting a rearguard action over a proposal I don't see as a good proposition long-term.'

'Would your father see it as one?'

'It's doubtful. Not that it makes any difference. He doesn't have a say in it these days.'

Claire said slowly, 'Is he likely to make a full recovery?'

'From the paralysis, maybe, but he has a heart condition too.' The tone was dispassionate. 'The specialist gives him a year at the outside.'

All the more could she understand and appreciate his reluctance to inflict further stress, Claire reflected, and all the less did she think of Scott. There was little enough excuse for Jill, but none at all for him.

It was touching midnight when they got to the house. There was no sign of Scott's car, and no light in any of the windows to indicate that Jill was already home.

'They must have had an accident!' exclaimed Claire worriedly. 'They were way ahead of us!'

'We'd have come across them if they had,' Ross reassured her. 'They'll have parked somewhere.' He switched off the engine. 'I'll wait with you till they arrive.'

Still not wholly convinced, Claire was only too glad to accept the offer. She certainly wouldn't be going to bed until the two of them did show up.

She made coffee, and took it through to the sitting-room where Ross was leafing through a magazine. Seated in the armchair that had been her father's favourite, legs comfortably stretched, he looked thoroughly at home.

'No milk, no sugar, isn't it?' she asked—a purely rhetorical question, as she remembered perfectly well from the previous evening.

'That's right.' He got up from the chair to come and take the cup from her, putting it down on the coffee-table as she poured one for herself, and sitting down at her side on the sofa. 'They'll get here any minute,' he assured her, registering her distraction. 'And I'll have one or two things to say to the pair of them when they do,' he added on a somewhat grimmer note.

'You and me both.' Claire was fluctuating between concern and anger. 'Surely to goodness they've had enough of one another for one night!'

'Scott never did know when enough was enough,' Ross said drily. 'Neither, it seems, does your sister. If this marriage lasts out the year, it will be a miracle. They're too much alike.'

'Opposites attract, similarities endure, isn't that what they say?' asked Claire, trying not to react too strongly to the criticism.

'Not when the similarities include total self-interest. There needs to be give and take in any partnership.'

'You might not think too much of your brother, but you don't even know Jill,' she protested.

The shrug was brief. 'It hardly takes any great insight. She wants what she wants when she wants it, regardless of who it might hurt.'

'That's not true!'

'Yes, it is. And you know it. She hasn't given you a moment's thought in all this.'

Sitting bolt-upright now, eyes emerald-bright, Claire said tautly, 'I think you'd better go.'

'You're sticking your head in the sand,' he rejoined, making no move to comply. 'I'm not suggesting that she doesn't have any redeeming qualities at all, any more than I'd condemn Scott out of hand. We all have our faults.'

'You surprise me.' Claire let the sarcasm rip. 'And what minor imperfections do you claim for yourself?'

'Impatience could be one of them.' He was beginning to sound as if he was suffering from it right now. 'If I was so wrong about her, she'd be here right now, not parked up somewhere doing what comes naturally with my brother while you worry about what might have happened to them.'

He put up a swift hand to catch the one that rose involuntarily from her lap, holding it in a grip of steel. 'I told you what would happen if you did that again. I wasn't joking, believe me.'

'Oh, I do!' The contempt in her voice was as much self-directed as aimed at him; losing control of her temper once was bad enough. 'I wouldn't put anything past you! It was all so much talk back there, wasn't it? You're no more reconciled to the marriage than you ever were!'

'I said we'd reached impasse on the subject, not that I was reconciled. There's a subtle difference.'

Too subtle for someone of her limited intellect to grasp was how the message came across from Claire's point of view. He was still holding her wrist, his grip tight enough to hurt a little. For a fleeting moment she was sorely tempted to swing the other hand up and across, but that would have simply served to underline her lack of imagination, as well as affording him the excuse to keep his word and return the compliment. She took a hold on herself, forcing the searing resentment under.

'Just go, will you?' she gritted.

The lean features tautened still further. 'I'll go when I've said what I want to say to the two of them, not before.'

'It isn't up to you to say anything!' Claire shot back at him, losing what composure she had managed to attain. 'Not to Jill, at any rate. This is our home, and *I* want you out of it. *Now*!'

The slam of a door cut off whatever response he had been about to make. Eyes glittering, he released her wrist. Jill put her head round the sitting-room door, looking anything but apologetic.

'I thought you'd be long gone,' she said to Ross.

He got abruptly to his feet, expression daunting. 'We've been waiting for you to get back. Where's Scott? And where the hell have you been?'

'Scott went home, and we just stopped for a few minutes to look at the moon,' she answered with asperity. 'We don't have to ask permission, do we?'

'No, you don't!' Claire was on her feet too, rage burning brighter than ever. 'Whatever else you have to say, Ross, save it for your brother! I'll handle this end, thanks!'

'Sure you will. With about as much success as you handled the last four years.' His tone was all the more cutting for its lack of volume. 'If you'd exercised a little more control, we'd none of us be in this position to start with.' He looked from one to the other of them, seemed about to continue, then apparently changed his mind, lifting his shoulders in a short, dismissive gesture more expressive than any words. 'I'll leave you to it.'

Jill stood aside to let him pass. 'Bye, big brother,' she said insolently.

Claire held her breath, but Ross ignored the wisecrack. A moment later the front door closed in his wake, leaving the two sisters facing each other across the few feet of carpet.

'That sounded like frustration to me,' said Jill speculatively. 'Did he try something on?'

'No, he didn't!' Claire was hurting too much from the accusations Ross had made to pull any punches. 'You've absolutely no shame, have you?' she accused her. 'You don't care how you make yourself look!'

'So we stopped for a goodnight kiss.' There was no defensiveness in Jill's voice. 'What's wrong with that?'

'I suppose you were only kissing earlier too, when you finished up with grass-stains all over your back. You realise that dress is ruined?'

Jill had the grace to flush a little. 'So what if it is? I'm hardly going to be short of a dress or two when Scott and I are married. I might even take some of your stock off your hands.'

'I don't stock maternity wear. That's all you're going to need for the next few months.'

For a fleeting moment the younger girl's face looked blank, then she gave a laugh. 'Of course. Silly me!'

She would be wasting both time and breath going on at her any further, Claire conceded, abandoning the reproaches as a lost cause. Jill was a past master at turning a deaf ear when it suited.

'What time is your appointment tomorrow?' she asked wearily.

'Appointment? Oh, you mean with the doctor?' Jill gave a vague shrug. 'Some time in the afternoon. Scott's taking me out to lunch first.' She put up a hand to smother a yawn. 'I'm going to bed. Are you coming?'

'As soon as I've cleared these away.'

Claire put the cups back on the tray with the coffee-pot, only now remembering the problem she still had to face with the car. She would have to take the bus in the morning, after all, and leave the tyre business for another day, she decided. Not an ideal arrangement, but better than getting up at the crack of dawn after a late night.

Not just a late night but a thoroughly upsetting one too, she thought painfully, carrying the tray through to the kitchen. Up until yesterday, Ross Laxton had been nothing more to her than a name on paper—a face known only through a newspaper photograph. Since meeting him, her whole life had been turned upside-down.

Those last biting remarks of his stuck in her craw. It was true that Jill had been left pretty much to her own devices during the hours between the end of the school day and Claire herself coming home, with the whole of Saturday free to do more or less as she liked, but only through necessity not neglect. Surely he could see that? In any case, who was he to say whether more super-vision would have made any difference to this particular outcome?

Scott was the real culprit, she told herself firmly, but found little comfort in it.

Monday turned out to be one of the busiest and most profitable days she had known in weeks. By closing time she was physically exhausted but jubilant too. If this kept up, she would be out of the wood—for the time being at least. For that, she told herself, she would suffer any amount of aches and pains!

Jill wasn't in when she finally reached home after queuing half an hour for a bus. Too weary to consider cooking anything, she made herself a salad sandwich, and took it out on to the small rear patio along with a glass of orange juice.

It was another lovely evening, with just enough of a breeze to stir the tree-tops. Mrs Johnson came to join her for a few minutes, full of plans for when her grand-child arrived.

It had to come out some time, Claire knew, and it might as well be now. The Johnsons would be coming to the wedding—or she hoped they would.

The older woman was silent for a moment when she told her the news, her pleasant, good-natured face registering sympathy and understanding.

'It happens, dear,' she said. 'I dare say it could have happened to Susan, too. Young people today don't look at these things the same way. At least Jill won't have to worry about the cost of bringing up a child. Everything is so expensive.'

Claire could imagine. Jill had every reason, she thought with irony, to count her blessings.

The invitation to the wedding was accepted without hesitation. 'We shan't need a card,' Mrs Johnson assured her.

Up until that moment, she hadn't given that side of it a thought, Claire realised. It was up to the bride's family to despatch invitations, of course, which meant getting in touch with Mrs Laxton to secure a list of names. Just family and close friends, she had said; that shouldn't amount to a great deal. Not that anything at all could be done until they had an actual date for the wedding.

Jill didn't arrive until gone ten, having been to the cinema with Scott. He didn't come in with her.

'So, how did it go?' asked Claire when her sister had failed to add the more vital piece of information. 'What did the gynaecologist have to say?'

Watching the news on television, Jill made a vague gesture. 'Oh, the usual stuff. Everything is fine.'

'He confirmed your reckoning?'

'Yes, that's right.' She was still riveted to the screen. 'I like this new newscaster, don't you? He's a dish!'

Claire sighed and gave up. If everything was all right, then that was all that mattered. Jill would gain more interest in the baby when she had some tangible proof of its existence. In the meantime, there were other things to think about.

'Did Mrs Laxton manage to fix a date for the wedding?' she queried.

'Yes. We're seeing the vicar tomorrow night.'

It was like pulling teeth! thought Claire, waiting in vain for more. She pressed the remote control's off switch, lifting exasperated brows at her sister as she looked round protestingly. 'Talk to me!'

'I *am* talking to you.' Jill sounded indignant. 'What else is there to say?'

Claire bit back a tart rejoinder. 'When is it to be?'

'Two weeks on Thursday. Three o'clock.'

Her half-day. That solved one problem at least. With the church organised, and the reception arrangements obviously in Mrs Laxton's court, that left only the invitations and their own personal transport—Jill would hardly want to travel to church in the Panda.

She would ring tomorrow about the invitations, she decided, and also discuss the question of costs. Perhaps it could be arranged for the reception bills to be sent directly to her.

'What about your dress?' she asked. 'Do you have any idea what you might like?'

'I thought you might like to design me one,' came the casual reply. 'Something really different.'

Design and make was what she meant, of course, and there was little enough spare time to do it in. All the same, Claire wanted to do it.

'I'd be glad to,' she said.

'One thing I shan't want is a veil,' declared Jill firmly.

A veil would hardly fit with the pattern beginning to take shape already in her mind's eye, Claire conceded. Something different it would certainly be.

Jill reached for the remote control and restored the picture, settling down in a chair to watch the rest of the newscast.

'By the way,' she said over a shoulder, 'Ross is giving us a honeymoon in the Maldives. Great, isn't it?'

All for effect, thought Claire contemptuously. Ross Laxton couldn't be seen to be a cheapskate over his only brother's wedding-present, no matter what his feelings on the subject. That Jill could bring herself to accept the offer so readily after what he had said the other night was no real surprise either. She obviously had her priorities all worked out.

'Terrific,' she agreed, keeping the satire low-key.

Later, in bed, she tried to come up with some ideas for her own wedding-present to the pair of them, but drew a blank. It was going to be a case of looking round and hoping to light on something, she decided in the end. No competition in monetary terms, of course; it would have to have value of another kind.

And Ross could go to hell, was her final thought.

CHAPTER SIX

WITH both the weather and her custom continuing to look good, the days seemed to fly by. Claire spent the majority of her spare time on the wedding-outfit, first in refining the initial design until she was satisfied with it, then in drawing the pattern and cutting out before commencing to sew the cream silk grosgrain which she and Jill had both considered ideal for the job.

It was a delicate task, with some of the stitching needing to be done by hand—a tiring one, too, although she didn't begrudge the effort. This might not be the wedding of the year, but it was still to be Jill's big day.

She telephoned Mrs Laxton on Thursday to ask about the guest-list. Like herself, the older woman sounded far from at ease with the subject.

'Considering the shortness of time, and the few people who will be coming to the wedding, I think it would be best if each of us issue our own informal invitations,' she suggested. 'If you could give me some idea of how many on your side will be coming back to the house afterwards...'

'About half a dozen,' Claire hazarded, not yet certain of Jill's plans in that direction. She hesitated before voicing the next question. 'About costs. Perhaps you could arrange for the bills to come directly to me?'

The reply was even more tentative. 'My husband wants to take care of all that himself.'

'That's good of him, but really not necessary,' Claire protested. 'Whatever Ross might have said, I *can* afford it!'

'It has nothing to do with Ross. Just something Hugh feels very strongly about, considering it was our younger son's behaviour that made it necessary in the first place. It will upset him very much if you refuse to allow it.'

Considering Mr Laxton's condition, that put her very much in a cleft stick, thought Claire resignedly. Aloud, she said levelly, 'Then all I can do is thank him.'

'Good.' The relief was evident. 'Then that seems to be that for the moment—unless you had something else you wanted to discuss?'

So far Jill hadn't mentioned the question of where they were going to be living after the wedding, and Claire couldn't, in all fairness, bring herself to do it now. 'No,' she said. 'That's it.'

'Then we'll see you in two weeks' time.'

She should be grateful, Claire supposed, ringing off. Even with custom looking up, she couldn't afford to become complacent about finances. All the same, now that she didn't have the wedding to pay for, the money put aside for Jill's education was going to be transferred into her name, she decided. At least that way her sister wouldn't be entirely dependent.

Scott was at the house when she got home. The two of them had been out somewhere for the afternoon, and were planning on attending an open-air concert later on, it transpired. In the meantime, they hadn't yet eaten.

Left to her own devices, Claire would have settled quite happily for a sandwich and coffee, but hardly felt able to fob Scott off with the same, but made a spaghetti bolognese, using a packet sauce for speed and disguising it with plenty of grated cheese. Beggars, she told herself in mitigation, couldn't be choosers.

To do him justice, Scott appeared to relish the simple meal equally as well as a more elaborate. Whatever his faults, he was impossible to dislike, Claire reflected, when he thanked her afterwards.

'Jill tells me you're going to the Maldives on honeymoon,' she said casually over coffee. 'That will be a nice start to married life.'

'And all courtesy of big brother,' he agreed. 'I'll say one thing for him—when he comes across, he does it in style!'

'Have you done a lot of travelling?' she asked.

'A fair amount. I intend taking Jill a whole lot of places she's never been before,' he added. 'There's a lot of world out there!'

And a life to make together right here, Claire wanted to say. With a baby on the way, they could hardly go gallivanting all over the world.

'There hasn't been a lot of opportunity for travel these last few years,' she said a little defensively instead. 'I couldn't just shut shop for a couple of weeks.'

'Couldn't someone have taken over for you?'

'Not without expecting to be paid. I don't have any friends with that much time on their hands.'

'Talking of friends,' chimed in Jill. 'I thought Andrew was due back Tuesday?'

Claire kept her tone even. 'He was.'

'You've seen him then?'

'Briefly, yes.'

Enlightenment dawned in her sister's eyes. 'You're saying he's ditched you?'

'It wouldn't occur to you that I might have ditched him, of course,' Claire returned drily.

'Not before time if you have. I never did think you were suited. All he could talk about was rugby,' she added, for Scott's benefit. 'He played every single Saturday!'

Scott grinned, pulling her close and holding her there as she wriggled and yelped. 'I'm all for a good tackle myself!'

Watching the two of them, Claire felt a pang of envy. They might be immature in many ways but they enjoyed what they had together. She and Andrew had lacked that essential spark.

Not that he'd taken his dismissal very easily last night. He'd finished up by calling her a stuck-up madam who didn't know a real man when she found one. He'd heard about the wedding by then, of course, and had taken it for granted that she had her sights set on Ross Laxton. If he only knew, she thought now, what little chance there was of her achieving such an aim even if she wanted to.

Jill and Scott were still wrestling on the sofa, the concert plans apparently forgotten. She left them to it, taking the coffee-cups through to the kitchen. The phone rang as she started to run water into the bowl. Wiping her hands, she went to pick up the kitchen extension.

'Is Scott there?' asked Ross without preamble.

Of all the people she might have expected to hear on the line, he hadn't been among them. It took her a second or two to recover her scattered wits.

'Yes,' she said shortly. 'I'll get him.'

'No point. Just tell him I want to see him here at the flat tonight, will you?' There was a pause, an easing of tone. 'Did you get the car fixed OK?'

'Yes, thanks. You were right about the tyres, of course,' she added with deliberation. 'It needed new all round.'

If he registered any sarcasm, he didn't rise to it. 'That must have cost you a pretty penny.'

'Oh, a mere fraction to what yours must cost *you*, I imagine.'

'The company pays for mine,' he said. 'You should be eligible for some tax relief yourself. Do you have an accountant?'

'No,' she admitted. 'I do my own accounts.'

'Not a good idea. You're probably missing out on several fronts. I could get our man to take a look at your books.'

'I can't afford to employ an accountant.'

The sigh signified impatience. 'I wasn't considering charging you. Can't you accept a simple gesture?'

Not, she thought, from him!

'Thanks, but no, thanks,' she said. 'I can manage my own affairs.'

'You're just about the most mule-headed female I ever ran across!' he exploded.

'Better than depending on charity.' She added pointedly, 'Was there anything else?'

'Nothing I'd care to say on an open line,' came the brusque response. 'Just give Scott the message.'

The receiver was replaced with some force, making her wince. She replaced her own instrument a little more carefully, refusing to regret the last remark. He'd hurt her too badly for it to be put aside just like that, no matter how generous the offer. Magnanimity was all too easy for someone in his position.

Scott looked unimpressed when she passed on the message.

'I'll not bother,' he said. 'It'll just be the same old lecture.'

'About what?' asked Jill.

He shrugged. 'Lack of interest in company affairs for starters.'

'And are you?' Claire queried. 'Uninterested, that is?'

The handsome features acquired a faintly condescending expression. 'I can find better things to do than sit around an office all day.'

'Like taking me out somewhere, for instance,' laughed Jill.

Claire bit her tongue. Scott was unlikely to appreciate any input from her. Jill was no help either. She obviously saw no reason why anyone should waste time working when they had no absolute need. Since meeting Scott, she seemed to have lost all sense of proportion.

Not a great deal she could do about it, Claire acknowledged wryly. Jill would turn a deaf ear to any criticism of her beloved.

With the wedding-outfit well on its way, and fed up with being indoors, Claire decided to devote the whole of Sunday to her own pursuits. The sky was clear when she got up at seven, though it wasn't as warm as it had been over the last few days. Better for walking, anyway, she reflected, determined not to be put off.

Dressed in jeans and a cotton shirt, she went downstairs to get the rest of her gear together. Her boots were three years old but still going strong, thank heaven. New ones were such a price! The rucksack had been her father's, and was coming to the end of its useful life, but it would last out the summer, she calculated, folding a lightweight anorak on top of the box of sandwiches and coffee-flask.

Despite the fact that the sky was beginning to cloud over, her spirits lifted with every mile as she drove out into the countryside proper. Kinder Scout was rough terrain—the climb to the plateau enough in itself to put off all but the dedicated walker. It was a week or two since she had been out, but she felt fit enough. Her calves and thighs would ache a little tomorrow, that was all.

She left the car in the parking area at the bottom of the village. Unusually, there didn't appear to be too many people about today. One small group headed up the road in front of her, but veered left at the top to take the alternative Pennine Way, while she kept straight on up the Grindsbrook route.

Sitting on a rock almost two thousand feet above sea-level a couple of hours later, she sipped a reviving coffee while viewing the broad lush valley spread out below. It was best seen in sunlight, but the lowering clouds couldn't detract from the overall grandeur.

She loved it up here, Claire reflected. Civilisation, with all its attendant problems, seemed light-years away. Apart from one solitary climber coming up the same rough path which she had trodden, there was no one in sight.

The man approaching had his head bent as he judged his way over the tumbled rocks below the summit. Wearing boots and anorak, with a rucksack on his back, he was obviously a serious walker.

A familiar one, too, she realised suddenly, feeling her heart give an almighty jerk as the dark head lifted to view the final ascent. Of all the places he could have chosen to walk, why, oh, why had he decided on this one today of all days?

She almost dropped her flask in her hurry to pack it away again, fastening the rucksack's clips with fingers made clumsy by haste. He would have seen her sitting here, but he might not have recognised her.

It was a toss-up as to whether he would be following the rim or heading for the Downfall. She opted for the Downfall herself, for the simple reason that she could soon drop out of sight among the dips and hollows of the peat bogs.

The wrong choice, she realised bare minutes later when she looked back to see the dark blue anorak as it hove into view. He was covering the ground at a fast pace, seemingly intent on catching her up—a purpose confirmed by the lifting of an arm in a signal to wait.

Claire did so, because there was no point in trying to outpace him. She met the grey eyes with a carefully neutral expression as he came up.

'You're taking a risk, coming out on your own,' he said, with a crisp authority that raised her hackles at once.

'*You're* on your own,' she returned pointedly.

'The worst I might suffer is a fall, and the centre knows I'm up here.' The pause was deliberate. 'They didn't say anyone had reported in ahead of me.'

Claire could have kicked herself. She recognised the sense in what he was implying; she just hadn't thought about reporting her intended route.

'I know Kinder like the back of my hand,' she claimed, not about to acknowledge the error. 'I've been coming up here for years without getting lost.'

Ross said something short and sharp under his breath. 'That's only part of it, and you know it,' he clipped. 'Any woman on her own way out here is simply asking for trouble. It never occurred to me that you'd be reckless enough to do it.'

She wasn't usually, she could have told him. The other members of the small mixed group she normally walked with had all been following other interests today, leaving her with a choice between staying home or taking her chances.

'I refuse to let myself be governed by the remote chance that some man is going to jump on me,' she retorted instead. 'I can take care of myself, thanks!'

Ross ran a slow and meaningful gaze over her. Her hiking-boots afforded her no more than an inch of extra stature, bringing her on a level with the centre of his chest. The jeans and anorak were hardly flattering but failed to disguise her fine-boned femininity.

'You reckon?' he said.

Suddenly conscious of her wind-whipped hair and face bare of make-up, Claire fought to maintain her composure such as it was. She wasn't out to make any impression. What did it matter how she looked?

'I reckon,' she stated unequivocally, 'a good kick in the right place works wonders.'

'Always providing you get to land it,' Ross returned drily. 'As we're obviously making for the same place, we may as well walk together.'

'It's a free country.' She did her best to sound as if she couldn't care less either way. 'I can't tell you where to walk.'

He took a couple of quick steps and seized her by the arm as she started to turn away, bringing her back round to face him. This close he towered over her.

'Look,' he said, 'the other night I was good and mad and perhaps said a great deal more than I should have done. I'm usually pretty even-tempered, but you...' He paused, viewing her stormy eyes and set features with resignation. 'All right, have it your own way, but like it or not you're stuck with me for the rest of the day.'

'As I said, it's a free country, and I can't stop you walking where you want to,' she responded curtly. She looked down pointedly at the hand still clasping her arm. 'If you'll remove that, please.'

'Not until you quit being so damned awkward!' Ross both looked and sounded exasperated. 'Women on their own in isolated areas are at risk; it's an unfortunate fact of life. You wouldn't be the first to discover it the hard way.'

He was right, she knew. It had happened to others, it could equally well happen to her. Devoid of other human life though the bleak landscape appeared to be at present, there was no saying who might be lurking in the gullies.

'That's better,' he said, when she failed to come back with some smart retort. 'Now, supposing we bury the hatchet the whole way?'

Claire lifted her shoulders in a gesture meant to convey indifference. 'Fine by me.'

He let it go at that. Releasing her, he fell into step at her side, adjusting his stride to accommodate her shorter one. After a few minutes, during which he made no attempt at conversation, and feeling anything but at ease with the silence, she made a supreme effort to dissemble.

'I didn't take you seriously about the hiking.'

'I realised that,' he said. 'Just goes to show how wrong first impressions can be. As a matter of fact, you're the first woman I've met who is interested in this form of exercise.'

'The others too sophisticated?' she suggested with satire.

He laughed. 'Not the kind to go bare-faced, at any rate.'

'I never wear a lot of make-up.' Claire refused to allow any hint of defensiveness to creep into her voice.

'With your skin you don't need to. Redheads seem to be particularly fortunate that way.'

Any gratification she felt at the unexpected compliment was overshadowed by the descriptive term she hated. 'I am not,' she declared, 'a redhead!'

'Copper-top, then,' he amended imperturbably. 'Whichever, it suits your temperament. You've one hell of a temper! Makes a man fear for his life!'

She snorted derisively. 'Like Goliath feared David!'

'Ah, but look what happened to him. Size isn't everything.'

It is when it's lacking, she thought, missing her heels.

'Did Scott call in the night you rang?' she asked after a moment.

Ross accepted the change of subject smoothly. 'No, he didn't. Nor have I had much opportunity to collar him since. He hasn't been to the office in days.'

'I know.' Claire felt guilty by very virtue of her relationship with the root cause of that defection. 'He and Jill seem intent on covering every known source of entertainment between here and the coast in both directions.'

'So I gathered.' He shot out an arm and caught hold of her as she stumbled over a stone, hauling her upright. 'Steady!'

'That's what I get for not looking where I'm going,' she said shortly, vibrantly aware of the tensile strength in the fingers gripping her arm. 'Thanks.'

'You've gone all prickly again,' he observed, letting go of her. 'Would you rather I'd let you fall flat on your face?'

Claire felt her colour mount. 'No, of course not. I was annoyed with myself for being so clumsy, that's all. Sorry if it came across that way.'

'You have quite a hang-up about being *petite* don't you?' His tone was matter-of-fact. 'You shouldn't have. You're in perfect proportion for your height.'

'Same as a Barbie doll!' she quipped, wishing he weren't quite so perceptive.

'And nearly as dumb if you let the lack of a few inches affect you.'

She said tartly, 'You don't believe in pulling your punches, do you?'

'Only when I'm fighting out of my weight. You can give as good as you get any day of the week.'

Humour overtook her. 'I suppose I could always stamp on your toes.'

'Not in those great boots.' He was grinning himself. 'We'll stick to the verbals.'

It became easier after that, although there was still an element of strain under the banter—on Claire's part, at least. She could never feel totally at ease with someone who made her feel the way Ross did, she admitted ruefully. Whatever else she might think of him, the attraction hadn't diminished one iota.

They weren't alone on the plateau. Figures were moving across the near horizon. The cloud had lowered still further, casting something of a pall over the rough-hewn landscape. They would have to keep an eye open, she reckoned, knowing the swiftness with which the weather could close in up here. Ross would know it too, of course, although he didn't appear to be concerned at present.

If she was honest about it, having him with her did afford a certain sense of security, she conceded, darting a glance at the tall figure pacing at her side. There were times when self-sufficiency had to give way to common sense.

Although lacking any wind to whip the spray back over the top in its usual spectacular fashion, the curtain of water cascading over the Downfall was scenic enough, and the view beyond panoramic. They ate lunch while seated with their backs wedged comfortably against a rock overlooking the dizzy drop.

Ross had brought canned beer to drink, but readily accepted a cup of hot coffee from Claire's flask.

'I keep promising myself another shot at the Way,' he remarked idly. 'All two hundred and fifty miles. I did it ten years ago. Quite an experience.'

'Something I always wanted to do myself,' Claire admitted. 'Dad did it twice, but I was too young the first time and studying for exams the second, much to my disgust.'

'Maybe we should organise a joint venture.'

Hardly a serious suggestion, Claire reckoned. She gave a laugh. 'I'd need wheels to keep up! Anyway, it's just a pipe-dream. I could hardly shut shop for ten days or more just to go swanning off along the Pennine Way!'

'Have you had a holiday of any kind since you lost your parents?' asked Ross after a moment.

'Well…no.' She was reluctant to acknowledge the fact, fearing that he might think that she was angling for sympathy. 'One of the drawbacks to sole proprietorship,' she tagged on lightly.

'So why not take on a partner? That would infuse some capital *and* afford you a little more time for yourself.'

'Easier to say than to do. In any case,' she added staunchly, 'I'd prefer to make it on my own, if I do it at all.'

'You're an independent young woman all the way round,' came the dry comment. 'But it can be taken too far. At the risk of being told to mind my own business again, what about the long-term future? You don't contemplate going through life on your own, do you?'

'I don't contemplate marrying for the sake of it,' she countered.

'So there's no one special around at present then?'

The question had been casual; Claire answered as casually. 'No one worth mentioning. How about you?'

He laughed. 'I'm not about to leap into any marital beds either.'

'I'd have thought it about time you started thinking about it, if you're going to do it at all,' she said, on what she hoped was a suitably jocular note. 'After all, you're not getting any younger.'

'True,' he agreed. 'But a man's time-clock doesn't run out quite as soon as a woman's. Chaplin was still fathering children in his seventies.'

'You fancy emulating him?'

'Well, maybe not.' He tossed out the coffee-dregs, and handed back the cup, fingers briefly touching hers as she took it from him. 'Electric, isn't it?' he added softly when she jerked as if stung. 'The energy two people can generate between them would light a city at times.'

'Is that what they call a power line?' she quipped, and saw his grin come and go.

'You can joke all you like, but you can't get away from it. We strike sparks together.'

The sudden change of mood was disturbing in more ways than one. Claire hardly knew how to react. 'I doubt if I'm even your type,' she got out.

'I don't go for any particular type.' He took the flask from her and set it down on the ground, then put a hand along her jaw to bring her head round towards him. His eyes had heart-stirring tawny lights in them. 'I'm not sure what I expected to find when I came to the shop last week, but you were one big surprise, I can tell you. Knee-high to a grasshopper, and feisty as a bull terrier!'

'Hardly to be wondered at, considering what you sprang on me.' She was doing her best to retain some degree of level-headedness. 'I didn't even know Jill was seeing anyone special.'

'So I realised. Anyway, that's a side-issue.' His thumb was smoothing her skin, sending ripple after ripple of sensation down her spine. 'You're enough to drive a man round the bend, Green-eyes. One minute all cool and collected, the next a raging virago! Are you always so quick to fly off the handle, or do I rile you more than most?'

'You could say that.' She put up a hand to grasp his, staying the movement. 'Leave it out, Ross.'

'Why?' he asked. 'Are you trying to tell me the attraction is purely one-sided?'

She wanted to say yes, but it would have been too obviously a lie. He would have felt too many women tremble at his touch to be deceived.

'I think you're playing a very familiar game,' she said instead. 'Familiar to you, that is. Only I'm not one of the easy-lay brigade!'

'I'm sure of it.' His tone was mild. 'I wouldn't be interested if I'd thought you were.'

'But you wouldn't deny having that in mind?' she challenged.

'Making love to you?' He gave a smiling shrug. 'It's a natural enough aspiration. What it does take is two of like mind. This would hardly be the place I'd choose, anyway.'

'Meaning your seduction technique would suffer from lack of a handy bed?'

His mouth curved again, eyes glinting with amusement. 'You've a real high opinion of me, haven't you?'

He had dropped the hand, but the feel of his fingers was still there on her skin. Claire dredged up a smile of her own, lifting her shoulders in deliberate mimicry. 'I'd doubt if your bedpost is short on notches.'

'Not in this day and age. Moderation in all things.' He leaned back against the rock, expression easy. 'Like I said, it takes two. Persuasion isn't my scene.'

He had probably never needed to employ it, she thought, half regretting the swiftness of her rejection just now. What harm could a few kisses do? Trigger something in her which might not be so easy to back away from, came the small voice of caution.

He fired her senses with just a touch; given any further leeway at all, he could undermine every ounce of self-control she possessed. The thought that it might be worth it she quickly suppressed.

She repacked her rucksack and buckled it up, aware all the time of Ross's regard. Attracted he might be, but obviously not enough to make any further moves. Perhaps as well, she reckoned wryly. She had no great trust in her strength of mind where he was concerned.

The valley below was still clear enough. It was only when she stood up and glanced back across the plateau that she realised how bad conditions had become during the last half-hour or so.

'We'd better start making tracks,' she said urgently. 'It's coming in heavy.'

Ross got to his feet with alacrity, face tensing a little as he scanned the fast vanishing landscape. 'My fault,' he claimed. 'I forgot the first rule.'

'We neither of us kept a weather eye open the way we should have.' Claire swung the rucksack on to her back, all other concerns pushed aside by this more immediate one. 'Let's be thankful we didn't leave it any longer.'

With visibility already down to a few hundred feet, and worsening by the minute, it would have been impossible to know which way they were heading if it hadn't been for the track forged by the passage of countless feet over the years. Even so, there were parts where the ground was so badly eroded that the track itself became indistinct. But they were both carrying compasses and Ross referred to his several times to make sure that they were still *en route* for the southern edge.

It was a relief to reach the downward path at last, but the weather didn't let up on them even then. Starting light, the rain turned in to a solid downpour, sheeting across the valley.

Claire's anorak was old enough to have lost much of its proofing, and within minutes she could feel the damp penetrating through. Her trousers were already soaked from the run-off, and clinging to her thighs. She was only too thankful for the coat of wax oil which she had applied to her boots the night before; at least her feet were dry.

Ross was wearing a summer-weight waterproof, guaranteed to keep out all but the most torrential deluge. He hadn't bothered to pull out the concealed hood and his hair was saturated, the ends curling back on themselves. He looked, she thought, a little sourly, as if he actually enjoyed getting wet!

They found the village mist-free but deserted, the surrounding trees dripping forlornly. Ross called in at the information office to report a safe return before heading down the lane to the car park. By the time they reached it Claire was soaked through to the skin, and feeling like something the cat had dragged in.

There were few cars left. Too few. Gazing blankly at the space where she had left the Panda, she even wondered for a moment if she'd left it out on the lane after all—but only for a moment. Her memory wasn't *that* bad.

'My car's gone!' she exclaimed.

CHAPTER SEVEN

'THERE'S a police station right across the lane,' said Ross. 'Mostly unmanned, I think, but there might be someone there.'

Claire accompanied him numbly, still finding it difficult to accept. Her insurance would cover the loss, of course, but what about transport in the meantime?

He came to an instant decision on finding the tiny sub-station locked. 'There's no point hanging around here. You need to get out of those wet things. We'll report the theft on the car-phone.'

'My house-key was in the glove-box,' Claire remembered out loud. 'And Jill said she wouldn't be home until late. That's even providing she took her key with her.' She made a helpless little gesture. 'I'll have to break a window.'

'First things first.' Ross turned back towards the car park. 'I've a rug in the boot. You can get out of those things and wrap yourself in that.'

'You're wet, too,' she protested, moving with him.

'Only my trouser bottoms. I'm as dry as a bone up top.'

'I should have had my anorak re-proofed,' she acknowledged ruefully. 'Or bought a new one. I just didn't expect it to turn out as bad as this today.'

'Typical English summer,' Ross observed. Reaching the Mercedes, he opened the rear door. 'Get in and strip off. I'll get the rug.'

She took off her saturated jacket before sliding into the seat, and dropped it onto the car floor. Ross handed

her a large red and black-chequered travel rug, then went
round to get behind the wheel, having first removed his
own jacket.

As he had said, the short-sleeved shirt he was wearing
beneath was totally dry, unlike Claire's which clung to
her like a second skin. He picked up the car-phone and
dialled Directory Enquiries, obtained the number of the
nearest manned police station and dialled again, cradling
the instrument between shoulder and chin while he
reached into the glove compartment for paper and pen.

'Registration number?' he asked.

It took her a panicky moment to remember it, just in
time for him to jot it down before the call was answered.

She had to take off her boots in order to remove the
clinging jeans. They joined her anorak on the floor, along
with her sodden shirt. Clad only in bra and briefs, she
clutched the rug about her gratefully, listening to the
exchange.

'That's right, Edale car park,' Ross confirmed. 'Red
Panda.' He gave the registration number, along with details of name and address, listened for a moment, then
said a brief thanks and put the instrument back in the
holder. 'They're going to put it on report. They reckon
it will probably be found abandoned somewhere.'

'Is that all they're going to do about it?' she exclaimed indignantly.

'Not a lot more they can do, I suppose. Do you want
to stay there or come up front?' he asked without turning
his head. 'You can slide between the seats without getting
out again.'

And risk losing the rug in the process, she thought.
'I'll stay here,' she said.

'Right.' He straightened to fire the ignition, repo-
sitioning the mirror. 'You'll still need to fasten
your seatbelt.'

Claire had forgotten about that. Nor was it any easy task settling the belt over the rug. She must look like a trussed chicken! she reflected, with a quirk of humour all too quickly dispelled by the recollection of why she was in this position to start with. Whoever had taken the Panda should have their fingers rot and drop off! she thought wrathfully. Joy-riders, at a guess. It was hardly worth stealing for any other purpose.

The rain eased off after a few minutes, and ceased altogether when they left the valley. There was every possibility that it had been dry all day back home, Claire knew. The Dales had their own weather system.

She said as much to Ross, who laughed and agreed.

'Just think how dull total predictability would be, though,' he added.

That was certainly something he couldn't be accused of, she thought, recalling his totally unexpected approach up on the plateau. In the short time she had known him, she had run the whole gamut of emotions—with temptation playing an undeniable part for a moment or two. What he'd said up there regarding his own attraction to her, she had to believe, but it made no difference. A fleeting affair with Jill's brother-in-law-to-be was *not* on her agenda.

As more than half anticipated, the sun was shining when they approached the town. From the look of the roads there had been no rain at all, Claire reckoned.

'This isn't the best way,' she asserted when Ross turned off the main road on to another, lined with large Victorian houses. 'It's quicker to go straight through town.'

'I know.' His tone was easy. 'We're going to my place.'

'I need some dry clothes,' she protested.

'I can supply something—along with a hot shower to ward off any chill. Better than breaking into the house, wouldn't you say?'

'I'll probably have to do that in the end anyway,' she pointed out. 'When Jill says "late" these days, she means late!'

'We'll cross that bridge if needs be.' He was drawing up as he spoke, turning into a wide, tree-shaded driveway. 'This is it.'

Claire briefly contemplated demanding that he take her straight home, discarding the notion because it smacked too much of distrust. Whatever else he might or might not be, a rapist he certainly wasn't. She had already told him no go.

Like many others in the area, the house had been converted into flats. Ross had the whole of the upper floor, reached via a private stairway. Still wearing her socks, and clutching the rug about her, Claire found herself ushered into an elegantly furnished hall.

'The bathroom is over there,' he indicated. 'I'll look you out a shirt or something you can put on until your things are dry. There's a tumble-drier in the kitchen. And no,' he added, before she could speak, 'I don't do my own washing. I have a woman come in twice a week.'

'Only twice?' she said blandly.

He grinned. 'You're getting a mite too big for your boots, lady!'

She gave him a caustic look before going into the well-appointed bathroom with its corner bath and variety of thick white towels. There was a separate, glass-doored shower cabinet. She set the water running before dropping the rug on the floor and stripping off.

Standing under the deliciously warm cascade, with face upturned to the flow, some moments later, she failed to hear the bathroom door open again.

'I'll put this over the hamper,' Ross advised. 'It should cover everything vital.'

She could be no more than an outline through the patterned glass, Claire realised, but even so she felt exposed. She stayed motionless until the door had closed again. That he could be so casual about it indicated that this was by no means the first time that he had walked in on a bather. He might well have stripped off and joined her had she been more forthcoming earlier.

She shut off that train of thought and finished showering quickly, stepping out to wrap herself in one of the huge bath-towels. The white silk shirt which he had left draped across the linen-basket was obviously hand-made. Something a little less expensive would have been preferable.

Dried, she donned her briefs again but decided her brassière was too damp. The shirt silk was heavy enough not to be see-through, and she was hardly of a size to make support essential.

With the buttons fastened and the sleeves rolled back to her elbows, she took a critical look in the long mirror fastened to the back of the door. Their light tan enhanced against the white, her legs were bare from mid-thigh. No more revealing than the average mini, she reassured herself—a great deal less so than many, in fact. In any case, Ross was hardly going to be driven overboard by a few extra inches of leg.

What she needed now was her boots, she thought whimsically, striking a pose. That would really take care of it!

Thickly carpeted throughout, the floors presented no problem for bare feet. She found Ross in a well-equipped kitchen at the far end of the hall.

'Omelette suit you?' he asked as she hovered uncertainly in the doorway.

'You don't have to cook anything for me,' she protested.

'I'm doing it for us both,' he returned equably. 'Cheese or plain?'

'Well, cheese, then—but let me do it.'

He gave her an ironic glance. 'That comes danger-ously close to sexism. Thanks, but no, thanks. I can handle it.'

Whether his use of the same phrase which she had used herself in refusing *his* offer of help the other night was deliberate or not, Claire couldn't tell. Whichever, it made her regret the way she *had* refused even more.

His mouth widened slowly as he viewed her. Towel-dried, and raked through with her fingers, her hair had sprung from its usual smooth styling into a copper cloud about her face, emphasising the brilliance of her eyes.

'You look like a wood nymph,' he commented.

'Today's latest fashion,' she quipped, determined not to be self-conscious about it. 'There must be *something* I can do.'

He indicated the winerack set in between two floor cupboards. 'You could be opening a bottle, if you like. You'll find a corkscrew in the drawer above.'

'Any particular one?' she asked, moving across to secure the corkscrew.

'Your choice. Those are all reds. If you prefer white, you'll——'

'Red will be fine.' She drew out the first to hand, failing to recognise the label. 'How about this one?'

'Good enough. You may as well pour it,' he added, tipping the beaten eggs into the waiting pan. 'This isn't going to take long.'

Claire held her breath as she drew the cork, but it came out clean. There were glasses in the cupboard close by. She poured the wine, savouring its fruity ambience. Good enough, Ross had said—a great deal more than that, she would have thought. Not that he would be likely to drink cheap plonk.

Seated across from him at the breakfast bar, she found it difficult to concentrate on food, good as the omelette and ready-made salad turned out to be. He had changed his damp jeans for a pair of close-fitting chinos in pale green, with a green and white-striped shirt open at the throat. The glimpse of dark chest hair fluttered her insides every time she looked up.

The wine was delicious, sliding down her throat like warm velvet. She was drinking it too fast, she knew, but it helped.

'I should try ringing home,' she said, when her plate was finally empty. 'Jill might have decided to come back early after all.'

'You never know.' Ross sounded ambivalent. 'There's a phone right by your elbow.'

There was no reply, of course. She hadn't really expected there to be. She replaced the receiver slowly, wondering just how long he intended waiting for the wanderer's return. If she had to break a window at all, it might just as well be sooner rather than later.

'My clothes must be dry now,' she said a little desperately, feeling his regard on her. 'I should at least get dressed.'

'I didn't put them in yet,' he confessed. 'What with getting changed and then starting this, I completely forgot. They're over there in the corner.'

'My fault more than yours,' claimed Claire hastily. 'I should have seen to it myself.' She slid from the high stool. 'I'll do it now.'

Ross had put the used crockery and cutlery in the dishwasher by the time she had finished. He had also poured more wine for them both.

'We may as well take this through and drink it in comfort,' he said. 'It could be a long wait.'

Far *too* long, she thought, but could see no immediate alternative.

The living-room was spacious, beautifully decorated and furnished without being in the least ostentatious. Claire curled herself into one of the deep club chairs, depositing her glass on the small table at her elbow, while Ross went to select a CD and fill the silence with an orchestral piece she recognised but couldn't put an immediate name to. It was still barely seven o'clock, she realised. Outside, the sun was shining, the world going about its regular Sunday evening business.

'How long have you lived on your own?' she asked when he came to take a seat on the nearby sofa.

'I moved out when I hit twenty-five,' he acknowledged. 'Though I've only had this place a couple of years.'

'It's very peaceful round here.'

'One of the reasons I like it.' He had his head back against the rest, one leg lifted comfortably across the other knee. 'The couple on the ground floor are quiet as lambs, except on the comparatively rare occasions when they throw a party. And as I'm always invited to those it's no problem.'

Claire kept her tone light, her eyes averted from the taut line of his thigh. 'Do you have parties, too?'

'Not yet, but there's always a first time.' He rolled his head to look at her directly, his expression hard to read. 'Would you come?'

'I'm not a party person,' she lied. 'Anyway, I doubt if you'd be short of guests. You must know a lot of people.'

'I'm acquainted with a lot of people; I count only a few as friends.' The pause was brief. 'It might not be a bad idea if you met the ones who'll be coming to the wedding beforehand. There's nothing worse than being faced with a sea of total strangers.'

'I thought it was only going to be a family affair,' Claire prevaricated.

'Family and close friends, we said. Neil and I have known each other since we were boys. He's like part of the family. So is Diane, his wife. Her mother and mine were in school together.'

'A close-knit circle,' she murmured, half to herself.

'Close, maybe, but not closed, if that's what you're thinking. Diane's a few years older than you, but you'd find her easy enough to get along with.' He smiled reminiscently. 'Always providing she didn't say anything to get across you, of course.'

'You make me feel a real shrew!' Claire complained.

'Rather sweet little creatures when they're not biting, I always thought.'

She pulled a face. 'I'm not sure I like that description any better. Maybe I should try altering my whole personality.'

'Not on my account. At the very least, life is never dull with you around.'

His tone was light, the words themselves hardly to be taken seriously. Claire laughed. 'I'll have that as my epitaph.'

She stole a swift glance at him when there was no immediate response, meeting his steady regard with a sudden jolting awareness. When he got to his feet she was too dry-throated to make any protest, regardless of what she knew was coming.

He scooped her bodily from the chair without effort, sitting down in it himself with her across his lap. His mouth was a source of endless pleasure. She ran her fingers up into the dark hair to pull him closer, not even attempting to pretend any longer. Why fight it? She had wanted this all along.

The scent of him in her nostrils was a stimulus in itself. Eyes closed, all clear thought arrested, she gave herself over to pure sensation, opening her lips to the gentle yet inexorable pressure, tremoring at the feel of his tongue exploring her inner softness, discovering an intensity of emotion which she had never experienced to the same degree before.

When he lifted his head she felt bereft. This close, the grey eyes had endless depths.

'Better,' he said softly. 'Anger was never an adequate substitute.'

'For what?' she asked, unsurprised by the husky quality in her voice.

His smile was slow. 'You know what I'm talking about. I want to make love to you, Claire. You want it, too. It's right there in your eyes.'

He brought up a hand to cup her jaw in much the same way as he had done earlier, causing her to tremor afresh as he traced a slow and infinitely tender passage with the very tips of his fingers along the firm line to the base of her ear. She knew about erogenous zones, but had never imagined that such a simple caress could elicit so delicious a sensation. She felt the curling warmth spreading from some central core to every part of her body, sensitising her skin to a degree where his lightest touch seared like a flame.

'I'm not going to bed with you, Ross,' she got out.

'But you want to,' he insisted softly. 'Don't you?'

She closed her eyes, gritting her teeth against the rising desire. 'We can't have everything we want.'

'We can if we want it badly enough.'

Opening her eyes again was a mistake. If nothing else betrayed her, they did. She made a half-hearted protest as he bent to kiss her again, but they both knew it was just a token gesture. Not just sex, came the fleeting thought. Not on her part, at least. The feelings he roused in her went far deeper than that.

The first tentative touch of his hand on her bared breast was earth-shaking. She shifted instinctively to allow the long lean fingers full access, wishing that she was bigger, fuller, more womanly.

'Beautiful,' he murmured reassuringly. 'Like ripe apples!' He bent to put his lips to the same spot, teasing her nipple into aching, tingling prominence with the subtle use of tongue and teeth. She clutched at him in a frenzy, hardly able to bear the exquisite sensation.

Fully unbuttoned, the shirt had fallen away, baring the whole of her body, but for the hip-hugging briefs, to his gaze.

'I was right,' he said softly. 'You are perfect. A pocket Venus!' He smoothed a hand down over her waist, smiling at the feel of her fluttering stomach muscles, eyes revealing his own growing desire. 'Mine are doing that, too.'

Claire doubted if he was experiencing quite the same degree of inner tumult. None of this was new to him. Regardless, there was no thought in her head of drawing back; she had come too far for that. Whatever regrets she might have later, it would be worth it for what she was feeling right now.

The pounding of blood in her ears increased three-fold as he slid the hand down beneath the band of her briefs to find her most intimate self with a touch like velvet. She had never allowed any other man the freedom to explore her this way, to discover her innermost secrets with such totality. She met his lips in passionate response, aware only of wanting, of needing. When he removed his hand she felt cheated, on the very verge of some even more earth-shattering experience.

'Don't stop,' she whispered. 'Not now. I don't want you to stop!'

'I don't intend to,' came the soft reply.

He stood up with no more effort than if she had been weightless, placing another searing kiss on her lips before starting to move. He was making for the bedroom, Claire realised, and she didn't care. There was so much more to come, and she wanted it all.

Empire-sized, the bed felt as wide as a football field. She lay there watching him take off his clothing through slitted eyelids, heart thudding like a trip-hammer.

He was built like a gymnast—upper body well-developed without being in any way gross, waist and hips taut and narrow. The explosion of hair on his chest tapered down to a narrow line above his hard-ridged stomach, then flared again to encompass the proud manhood. Already fully aroused, he made her tremble anew.

Totally without self-consciousness, he took her hand and guided her to him as he came down on the bed at her side, drawing in a deep shuddering breath at her touch. 'That feels so good!'

Emboldened, Claire allowed her instincts to take over, exploring him the way he had explored her, taking pleasure in his pleasure. She had never imagined herself as being so uninhibited, so utterly and completely free of restraint.

The sudden clamour of the telephone jerked every nerve in her body. Ross went rigid for a moment, swearing under his breath.

'Ignore it,' he said. 'It will stop.'

'I can't.' Her voice seemed to be coming from a long way off. 'It might be important.'

He swore again, and levered himself upright to take the receiver. 'Hello?'

From where she lay Claire could hear a woman's voice on the other end of the line, if not the actual words. She listened, frozen, to Ross's end of the conversation.

Whoever the woman was, he despatched her in short order, and with scant ceremony, but for Claire the castles had come crashing down. She sat up to rebutton the shirt with unsteady fingers, unable to look Ross in the eye when he turned back to her.

'This wasn't a good idea to start with,' she said thickly.

He took hold of her hand, stilling the movement. 'It was an excellent idea,' he declared. 'It still is.'

'No!' She tore the hand free, rolling away from him to slide off the other side of the bed and stand up, legs shaky. 'Just leave me alone, Ross!'

The skin looked stretched taut over his facial bones. 'You didn't want me to leave you alone a few minutes ago. You were as ready as I was to take it the whole way.'

'That was then,' she said. 'This is now. You've obviously enough women in tow without adding me to the list!'

'That's neither true nor fair.' He was making every effort to maintain a level tone. 'You were the one who insisted I answer the phone. If you've changed your mind, OK. Just don't try making me out to be an out-and-out profligate because of one unfortunately timed phone call.'

She *was* being unfair, Claire knew. Ross was a free agent. In a way, she supposed, she should be grateful to the unknown woman on the phone. She had saved her from making the biggest mistake of her life.

'I'm going home,' she declared. 'I'll call a taxi.'

He shook his head, face grimly set. 'No, you won't. Just give me a few minutes and I'll take you home myself.'

She made no answer to that, just left him sitting there.

Only when she had her jeans and shirt and was safely inside the bathroom did she start to take stock. Making love with Ross would have been wonderful while it lasted, for certain. Only, what would it have gained her? All he felt for her was the casual passion of any man for any woman who happened to appeal. More than she'd imagined, perhaps, but still nowhere near enough.

It was better this way by far, she decided hollowly. What you hadn't had you didn't miss.

He was dressed and waiting in the hall when she emerged. Glancing at him as he straightened away from the wall where he had been leaning, Claire had a vivid mind's-eye picture of the way he had looked a short time ago—an impression that was going to be with her a long time. She felt all churned up inside still.

Expression tightly controlled, he indicated the door. 'Let's go.'

They descended the stairs in silence. Claire waited until they were in the car and pulling away from the house before making any attempt to speak.

'I'm sorry if you're feeling frustrated,' she said, low toned, 'but it's for the best. I'm not on the pill, so we might even have finished up the same way Scott and Jill did.'

Ross kept his eyes front, face unrevealing. 'Seems you and your sister are pretty much on a par when it comes to taking precautions. I suppose I should think myself fortunate that I got the one with some scruples.'

'Jill isn't unscrupulous,' she returned, with what dignity she could muster. 'And when it comes to taking precautions——' She caught herself up, realising what she had been about to give away, and said instead, 'I didn't notice you taking any yourself, if it comes to that.'

'You didn't give me much of an opportunity.'

'I suppose,' she said shortly, 'you keep an ample supply ready in your bedside drawer!'

'You suppose quite rightly. Only fools take risks.'

'Only fools allow themselves to be lured by men like you in the first place!' Claire shot back at him. 'Like most, you just can't bear being turned down, can you?'

The lean profile looked as if it was etched in stone. 'If it hadn't been for that damned phone call, you'd have turned nothing down! You were as hot as they come.'

'And you'd know just how hot they do come, of course!'

They were out on the main road now, but the evening traffic was light. Ross drew into the roadside and sat for a moment with hands resting on the wheel before turning his head to give her a direct look. The grey eyes held no hint of warmth.

'This has gone far enough,' he said. 'I agree, the whole thing was a mistake, but it was one we both made. You're not a child, Claire. You had a very good idea of what was likely to happen.'

Face taut, she said thickly, 'I'd never have stayed if I'd realised you had that in mind all along. I gave you credit for being *something* of a gentleman.'

'I gave *you* credit for being above playing the last-minute withdrawal game. If it hadn't been the phone call, you'd probably have found some other reason to back out. Some women take pleasure in that kind of thing.'

The clipped tone he was employing made the words weigh even more. Claire could hardly breathe for the constriction in her chest.

'I'm not one of them,' she denied. 'The phone call made me realise how stupid I was being, that's all. It's different for you. A man doesn't need to feel anything more than the basic urge.'

'If that were true, I'd have one of those blow-up dolls.' Ross both looked and sounded thoroughly fed-up with the whole conversation. 'Let's just accept that you changed your mind. You're entitled.'

There was nothing more she could say, Claire conceded numbly as he put the car into motion again. Even if there were, she doubted if he would be prepared to listen. It was true too; she had changed her mind. Without any deeper feeling, on both sides, it would have been nothing more than an act. She had waited this long—why settle for so little now?

CHAPTER EIGHT

IT WAS some relief to turn the corner and see Scott's car on the drive. At least that was one problem out of the way.

Ross drew up at the gate, leaving the engine running. 'The police will contact you with any news,' he said. 'Don't forget to inform your insurance company first thing.'

'As you pointed out not so long ago, I'm not a child,' Claire responded shortly. 'I can handle my own affairs.'

The shrug was brief. 'Fine. I'll leave you to it.'

Bristling, she put her hand on the door-lever, then paused in sudden ashamed acknowledgement. She was acting *exactly* like a child. 'Sorry,' she said impulsively.

'That makes two of us.' There was no discernible softening of tone. 'You were right the first time. It should never have happened. Let's just agree to forget it.'

Forget it? With the images still engraved on her mind, the feel of his hands still on her body!

She got out of the car without answering, resisting with an effort the urge to slam the door on him. She was halfway up the drive before she heard the car pull away. That, she told herself hollowly, was that.

The front door was unlocked, but there was no sign of either Jill or Scott. Only when she heard the sounds from upstairs did she realise what was going on. Not that she had room to censure the two of them, she admitted wryly. They at least shared the same emotions.

They came downstairs together some minutes later, looking anything but discomfited to be caught out.

'I thought when you weren't here that you'd be gone for the whole evening,' said Jill somewhat obviously. 'You don't usually stay out this long hiking.'

'I know. It was such a lovely day.' Claire left it at that, trusting it would be enough to satisfy any lingering curiosity. 'Have you eaten?'

Scott grinned. 'Only the food of true love! Apart from that, I'm ravenous.'

'Me too,' agreed Jill.

'Then you'd better get yourselves something,' Claire returned. 'There's plenty of food in the freezer. I'm going to have an early night.'

She left the two of them standing there looking thoroughly nonplussed. It would do them good to fend for themselves for once. Ross was right, of course, she admitted. Jill was equally as self-centred as Scott. So far they were in accord, but heaven help the forthcoming marriage when the differences started to arise—as they surely would.

With the sun not yet set and the bedroom over-warm, sleep was out of the question. She tried reading a book, but couldn't concentrate. Eventually she gave it up, and sat looking out of the window on to the rear garden.

They were having a barbecue next door, and obviously enjoying every minute. Susan was there with her husband, her maternity dress already bulging large. Several of the neighbours too, Claire noted. No doubt she and Jill would have been invited had they been home.

Last month, at this time, life had been relatively simple, she reflected. Now Jill was pregnant, and she was more than halfway in love with a man she had alienated beyond hope of redemption. A total mess didn't even begin to describe it.

The police telephoned before she left for the shop on Tuesday morning, to say that the Panda had been found abandoned on some waste ground. The only damage appeared to be a broken door-lock.

'You've been lucky,' the duty sergeant advised. 'Someone just wanted a ride home out of the rain. Can you collect it right away, or do you want it taking to the pound for safety? You'll have to pay the towing charge if you do.'

Claire did a quick calculation. The area where the car had been dumped could be reached by bus, but it was obviously going to take time, which she didn't have, to get there. On the other hand, towing charges were likely to be high. The shop would just have to open late for once, she concluded.

'I'll fetch it now,' she said. 'And thanks.'

'All in a day's work, madam,' came the dry reply.

Jill was still in bed when she left the house. Scott had been here until gone midnight again last night. What plans they might have for today, Claire neither knew nor cared very much at the moment. Once they were married, Jill would be outside any influence from her anyway, so what was the point?

It took her over an hour to reach the car, and all the time she was hoping that it wouldn't have vanished again. With no door lock, there was every chance.

The waste ground appeared to be a regular local parking place, with the Panda only one of a dozen or more vehicles. Claire was relieved to find her house-key undisturbed under a pamphlet in the glove-box, although it had been unlikely that anyone but a professional with contacts in the DVLC would have been able to obtain her address.

She finally reached the shop at eleven, after dropping the car at the garage to have a new lock fitted. How many customers she might have lost in the interim she didn't care to imagine.

There were several letters on the floor under the flap. Scanning through them, she felt her breath catch in her throat on sight of the all too familiar name and logo. She had been expecting the lease renewal, of course, but its coming today, more than a week early, seemed like an omen.

She read the contents twice, unable to believe them the first time. A twenty per cent rise in rent would cripple her! This was Ross's doing, of course, she thought furiously. His way of paying her out for the dent she'd put in his precious masculine pride! Well, she wasn't about to take this lying down either!

Turning the door-sign back to 'Closed', she made for the office and snatched up the phone, dialling one of the numbers shown on the letterhead. The woman who answered responded to her demand to be put through to the chairman's office with typical polite evasion, but Claire was having none of it.

'Just tell him it's his sister-in-law, and he'd better speak to me!' she snapped.

There was a pause before the receptionist answered, speculation rife in her voice. 'Hold the line, please.'

Had there been any canned music played while she waited Claire would have exploded. As it was, she could barely contain the blazing anger. The sound of Ross's voice on the line was a further stimulus.

'You're being a little premature, aren't you?' he said coolly. 'It's another ten days to the wedding.'

'If it were up to me, it wouldn't be happening at all,' she retorted. 'Even then, Jill will be your sister-in-law, not me, thank heaven!' She gave him no time to respond. 'I hope you're satisfied!'

'What are you talking about now?' He sounded genuinely perplexed.

'You know damn well what I'm talking about! Another twenty per cent will finish me—you know that too! I've no doubt you've made it your personal business to ferret through every last particle of my affairs!'

'Just hold it right there.' The tone was forceful. 'If it's the lease renewals you're on about, you're talking to the wrong man.'

'Like hell I am!' Claire was too incensed to give reason a chance. 'You're a vindictive, petty-minded swine, Ross!'

The connection was cut with a thud as the receiver went down, leaving her suspended on a breath. For several numbed seconds she continued to hold the instrument to her ear, until the dialling tone was interrupted by a recorded voice advising replacement of the handset.

Only when she had done that did her mind start to function on a saner level. Hers wasn't the only lease in the area due for renewal, and was unlikely to be the only one with a rent rise. She picked up the envelope again, looking at the date stamp with a suddenly sinking heart. It wasn't unknown for even first-class post to take more than the one day to reach its destination, of course, especially when posted on a weekend.

She sank down into the chair feeling suddenly sick. She'd gone off like a firecracker as usual, allowing herself no time to consider. How could she have imagined for a moment that Ross would stoop so low, even given the opportunity? He simply wasn't that type.

No use sitting here wallowing in self-recrimination, she told herself bleakly. She had a shop to run. The rent rise would have to be met one way or another if she wanted to continue in business at all. Her overdraft was running at its limit, but the bank might be prepared to extend it. She could try, at least.

She had just dispatched a customer, some forty minutes or so later, and was contemplating making a cup of coffee, when Ross walked in. Tight-lipped, he flipped the 'Closed' sign around and pulled down the door-blind before turning to view her with eyes like cold steel.

'Now, supposing we talk this through like rational adults?' he clipped.

Wearing dark grey pinstripe, his shirt snowy beneath, he was every inch the executive, and heart-jerking with it. Claire couldn't find the words she needed.

'You're losing me custom,' she said instead as a woman paused outside to study the window display.

He made no move. 'Tough! The door stays closed until we've got things sorted out to mutual satisfaction. The lease——'

'I know.' Claire forced herself to look him in the eye. 'It wasn't your doing—not directly, anyway.' She made a wry gesture. 'I'm sorry for flying off the handle the way I did. I didn't stop to think it through.'

'Just took it for granted that I was on a personal vendetta.' There was no melting of the ice. 'The time element aside, I'm not in the habit of taking revenge on a woman because she happens to say no.'

Back against the mirrored cabinet, Claire said softly, 'I don't imagine you're often faced with the problem.'

The dark head inclined in sardonic acknowledgement. 'Let's stick to the matter in hand, shall we? As I was saying, the lease renewals aren't my personal concern, but I'll look into it.'

'You don't need to.' She was standing straight now, doing her best to regain some dignity. 'I don't want any special treatment.'

Ross studied her for a lengthy moment, his eyes following the figure-skimming lines of her coral dress with an expression that raised flags of colour in her cheeks. 'You said the increase would finish you.'

'That was off the top of my head, when I wasn't thinking straight. I can handle it.'

'How exactly?'

Green eyes registered a fleeting spark. 'That's my business.'

'In other words, you'd go under rather than admit you're in difficulties.'

'So what would you expect?' she flashed, with a renewal of her normal spirit. 'You can hardly have my rent reduced without doing the same for all the other lease-holders. Not without setting tongues wagging, at any rate.'

'They'll be doing that already. The wedding is no secret, but sisters-in-law don't usually come in advance. There's every chance that the line was accidentally left open.'

Claire felt her face go hot again. She tried desperately to recall exactly what she *had* said. A whole lot of invective, for sure.

'I'm...sorry,' was all she could find to say, for what seemed like the umpteenth time.

'So you should be.' Ross waited a moment, as if in anticipation of something more from her, then shrugged and turned away to lift the blind. 'I'll get out of your way.'

'Don't.' The word was jerked from her by a force stronger than damaged pride. 'Just leave it down, please.'

He looked back at her, observing the indrawn lower lip and rigid stance without noticeable change of expression. 'Do you want me to go?'

She shook her head. 'I'm such an idiot,' she muttered.

'No, you're not.' The lines of his face had relaxed a fraction. 'A firebrand, perhaps, but far from a fool. Sunday night was my fault. I should have known better.'

'So should I.' She looked at him with veiled eyes, afraid of revealing too much. 'I acted like some silly schoolgirl.'

Humour touched the strong mouth. 'Not all the time.'

She blushed furiously as memory overtook her. Not all the time indeed!

Watching her, his expression altered again, taking on a certain comprehension. 'You've never done it before, have you?'

There was little point in attempting to deny what must have been patently obvious, Claire conceded. She shook her head.

'Mind if I ask why not?'

'Probably because I haven't met anyone I wanted to do it with. Not enough, at any rate.'

'But you wanted to with me.' It was a statement not a question. 'I find that very ego-boosting.'

From somewhere she conjured a smile. 'As if you needed it. Anyway, it didn't get very far.'

'The blame for that to be laid directly at British Telecom's door.' He paused, then added levelly, 'It might be best if we keep the relationship on a strictly friendly footing from now on.'

Pride formed the words for her. 'I think so too.'

'No reason why we shouldn't stick to the arrangement we made to have you meet Diane and Neil before the wedding, though. How about dinner Friday—providing they can make it?'

Claire recalled no specific arrangement, and felt too down to argue the point. A friendly footing would be better than no contact at all.

'Fine by me,' she said, trying for a level note herself. 'And...thanks.'

He lifted a quizzical brow. 'For what?'

'For coming over. You could have just ignored the whole thing.'

'Not the way you dished it out. Speaking of which,' he added, 'call me a swine again, and I might just turn into one.'

'I'll make sure to wipe it from my vocabulary,' she promised.

He laughed. 'I'll be in touch.' On the point of turning away again, he paused once more—in recollection this time. 'Any news of the car, by the way?'

Claire had almost forgotten the morning's previous disruption. It seemed pretty tame in comparison. 'I got it back,' she acknowledged. 'Just a broken door-lock. It's being fixed right now.'

'That's great. Saves a lot of hassle.' His lips tilted ironically. 'A wonderful world, isn't it, when we have to be grateful to thieves for not doing too much damage!'

Right at that moment, watching him out of the door, Claire couldn't have cared less about the car.

Friendship wasn't what she wanted from him—not on its own, at any rate. If she hadn't been so utterly infantile the other night she would at least have had that much to look back on, she thought, depressed—and there would quite probably have been more of it to come. How many got to her age these days without having indulged in at least one affair along the way? Life was for living, not hanging around waiting for a Mr Right who might never appear.

None of which made the slightest difference where Ross was now concerned. He'd obviously lost interest in any further pursuit along those lines. It said a lot for his character that he held no grudge against her—especially in light of what she had said to him on the phone a while ago. She wasn't sure she could have been quite so magnanimous had the positions been reversed.

But then, *he* would probably not have lost control of his temper in the first place, came the wry acknowledgement. The other night had indicated as much. Where some men might well have felt provoked into forcing the issue, he had reacted with commendable restraint. She could admire him for that too.

The afternoon passed slowly, and not too profitably. She made an appointment to see her bank manager the following week. It was a long shot but worth a try. If he refused, she would simply have to think of something else.

Much to her surprise, she found Jill not only in but alone when she arrived home. Snappy too, when asked what had happened to the boy wonder.

'We simply decided to have an evening apart, that's all! Any reason why we shouldn't?'

'None at all,' Claire returned mildly, wondering if that first clashing of interests had already happened. 'A change is as good as a rest.'

Her sister's pretty face failed to lighten. 'Trust you to trot out that old cliché!'

If she didn't know better, she would put the shortness of temper down to PMT, thought Claire, leaving her to simmer on her own while she went up to change. Jill had been prone to such attacks over the last year. Perhaps it was possible that the hormonal changes which triggered the condition were much the same as those taking place in various stages of pregnancy, she mused, stripping off her dress and donning jeans and a shirt instead. If so, Scott could look forward to squalls in the forthcoming months.

The wedding-outfit was finished, except for a final stitch or two. She would have liked Jill to try it on one last time, but she showed little interest.

'It fits fine,' Jill said. 'The things you make always do. It's bad luck, anyway, before the wedding.'

'Only if the groom sees you in it.' Claire waited a brief moment before adding gently, 'The first three months are always the worst.'

'How would *you* know?' came the peevish retort.

'It's common knowledge.' Claire refused to be provoked. 'If you're feeling bad, I'm sure the doctor would
prescribe something.'

'I'm not sick, and I don't want anything!'

Sighing, Claire gave up. It was only to be hoped that
the mood wouldn't last too long, or the wedding guests
were going to wonder just what Scott had let himself in
for—to say nothing of the Laxtons themselves.

She had never once asked Ross how his father was
these days, she realised regretfully. Scott's word was
nothing to go on. She doubted if he would notice any
change either for the better or for the worse, short of
the most radical.

There had been no mention, either, of any change of
plan regarding living accommodation, although she was
pretty sure that Ross would have kept his promise to talk
to his brother about it. That alone might have something to do with Jill's state of mind.

Wednesday brought rain, and a further dampening of
spirits. Not that a few customers more or less were going
to make all that much difference in the long run, Claire
accepted. She might have done better all round by
catering for the wear-once-and-throw-away end of the
market from the start, she reflected, not for the first
time. If she had had the room, she might even have tried
diversifying, but space was limited as it was.

What would be would be, she concluded, refusing to
give way completely to depressive speculation. If this
venture finally failed, she would simply try something
else—although what exactly she had no idea.

The weather had cleared around lunchtime, but even
this didn't appear to have tempted too many people into
coming to town. Wednesday was always a fairly quiet
day at the best of times. Mid-week blues, Claire always
called it.

Coming out from the office, on hearing the bell jingle, to find Ellen Laxton standing there was something of a shock.

'Hello,' she said. 'This *is* a surprise!'

The older woman smiled and shrugged. 'I thought it about time the two of us got together. The telephone is no real substitute.'

For what? Claire wondered. 'Perhaps you'd like to come through to the office,' she invited. 'It's not very big, I'm afraid, but better than standing around in here.'

'Actually, I'd like to have a look at your stock,' Ellen returned. 'A friend of mine called in last week and found just what she was looking for. She said you had some excellent lines.'

'I try to cater for as wide a taste range as possible.' Claire was running a mental check of last week's customers, so far as she could remember them, and attempting to work out which it might have been. Not that there were so many to choose from. 'Would it be a Mrs Wendover, by any chance?' she hazarded.

'That's right. Anna Wendover.' Ellen was obviously surprised. 'Do you know all your customers by name?'

Claire laughed and shook her head. 'Only the regulars, and there aren't very many of those. Mrs Wendover paid by gold card. I don't get too many of those either.'

'I shouldn't imagine you'd want them, considering the percentage you have to pay the company for the privilege,' was the shrewd comment. 'It must cut quite deeply into your profit margin.'

'Fairly.' It was as far as Claire was prepared to go in discussing her financial affairs.

Ross had put his mother up to this, she suspected. It was even on the cards that he had been the one to suggest Candice to Mrs Wendover, or at least to have implanted the idea. It shouldn't matter how business was procured, providing the customer went away satisfied, said the voice of reason, but she still felt just a little patronised.

'Do feel free,' she invited, refraining from offering any help as she normally would.

Ellen took the hint, walking slowly along the rails lining either side and the far end of the long but narrowish room, her heels sinking into the mid-blue carpet that had cost the greater part of the total decorating and fitting-out budget at inception, but which had paid dividends in still looking almost like new four years later.

The blue and white-striped wallpaper, small crystal chandeliers and rosewood-framed cheval mirrors all tied in to present the kind of gracious ambience Claire had wanted. It was perhaps a little off-putting for some, she had realised since, in its suggestion that everything must cost accordingly—and getting people through the door in the first place was half the battle.

'You have a very good eye for style,' Ellen commented. 'But then you would have. Ross said you were halfway through a design course when your parents died.'

Jill might have mentioned it at some time to Scott, who could have passed it on, Claire supposed, unable to recall talking about it with Ross himself.

'Yes, I was,' she said briefly.

Ellen gave her a swift glance. 'You never thought of taking it up again?'

'I couldn't afford the time.'

'But you are designing and making Jill's wedding-gown, I understand?'

Gown, thought Claire humorously, was something of a misnomer.

'Well, yes,' she agreed. 'But that's just a one-off. I'm nowhere near good enough to start thinking along commercial lines, if that's what you're suggesting.'

Ellen smiled, not in the least put out. 'Just a thought.' She unhooked a Chanel-style suit in deep gold trimmed with black braid. 'May I try this on?'

Claire bit back the response which sprang to her lips. It might very well be just a gesture, but that was no reason to throw it in the woman's face. The suit was expensive, and certainly on a par with the quality of the pale beige one which Ellen Laxton was wearing at present.

'The dressing-rooms are over here,' she said instead, pulling back a curtain to reveal the somewhat limited space. 'You might find it easier to come out again for an all-round view.'

The suit looked good on, she had to admit some few minutes later. Tall and slim, Ellen carried clothes well. Claire said as much, receiving a gratified smile in reply.

'I really like this,' she declared, sounding genuinely enthusiastic. 'It isn't a colour I'd normally go for, but it's about time I tried something new. I might even wear it to the wedding.' She laughed. 'At least you shouldn't have any trouble finding something.'

Claire hadn't even thought about what she was going to wear as yet. Nothing from stock, for certain—she couldn't afford it.

'I feel so bad about it all,' she said on impulse. 'Especially considering Mr Laxton's condition. It can hardly have helped.'

'Actually, he's a little better,' Ellen returned. 'His speech is coming back, which makes things so much easier for him. As to the other——' she lifted her shoulders '—these things happen. Jill is a lovely girl. I'm sure she and Scott will be very happy.'

'Jill is a self-willed brat,' Claire stated frankly. 'My fault, I'm afraid. I've tended to let things slide a bit where discipline's been concerned.'

'Hardly surprising when you were so young yourself at the time you had to start looking after her.' The tone was sympathetic. 'Scott leaves a lot to be desired when it comes to responsibility too, if it comes to that, and he's old enough to know better.

'I'm only too thankful that Ross turned out the way he did. Not that I wouldn't be even happier if he'd settle down himself. It's hardly for lack of opportunity, after all.'

That remark seemed to indicate the possibility of someone waiting in the wings for Ross to decide the time was right, thought Claire as the other woman disappeared into the dressing-cubicle again.

So what of it? she asked herself hardily. She had no claim on him. Getting over him might be a great deal easier if she never saw him again, but that was hardly going to be possible, even if she backed out of this dinner-date which he had already confirmed. She would just have to live with it.

CHAPTER NINE

SCOTT held his stag night on Friday, a decision Claire found surprisingly sensible. With Jill's moods fluctuating the way they were still, it was probably as well for the two of them to be apart for a while anyway, she decided.

She had left it until the last minute to mention the dinner-date with Ross and his friends, aware of the likely reaction. She wasn't disappointed.

'If anyone should be meeting these people it should be me, not you!' exclaimed Jill peevishly. 'I'm the central figure in all this, after all.'

'They're hardly your age group,' Claire pointed out. 'You'd be bored out of your mind.'

'They're hardly yours either, if it comes to that. Ross is at least ten years older than you are.'

'*Only* ten,' Claire corrected, and wished she hadn't as the hazel eyes took on a sudden light of suspicion.

'You fancy him, don't you?' she said on an accusatory note. 'For heaven's sake, Claire, he's nothing but a big, bossy bully!'

Claire couldn't stop the smile from forming. 'Nice alliteration. All that education wasn't wasted after all.'

Jill's sense of humour appeared to have taken the same route as her good temper. 'Don't make fun of me!' she snapped. 'I'm sick of people treating me like some stupid kid!'

'So stop acting like one,' Claire countered, losing her own patience. 'Ross only suggested this so I wouldn't

be meeting too many total strangers on the day. A
thoughtful gesture, that's all.'

'But you still fancy him.' It was a statement now, not
a question. 'It won't do you any good. Scott says he has
women all over the place!'

'Scott has no room to talk when it comes to moral
values. At least Ross hasn't got anyone pregnant!' Claire
broke off abruptly, ready to bite off her tongue as she
saw the hazel eyes go suddenly dark. 'Oh, Lord, I'm
sorry, Jill! That was mean.'

For a moment the pretty young face crumpled, as if
on the verge of tears, then it set again, chin jutting
fiercely. 'I don't care *what* you say. I don't care what
anyone says! We're going to be married. That's all that
matters! Just leave me alone, will you?'

Claire stood irresolute as Jill flung herself down on
the sofa, wanting to go to her and offer comfort, yet
knowing how any such overture was likely to be received
at the moment. When it came to temperament, there was
little to choose between the pair of them, she admitted
wryly.

The best thing she could do was to take Jill at her
word for now, and leave her to come round in her own
time. That was what she would have wanted herself in
similar circumstances.

In the meantime, she still had to shower and dress
before Ross arrived, as arranged, to pick her up at eight.

She had chosen to wear another of her own cre-
ations—this time a trouser-suit in a fine, off-white Italian
knit. He regarded her approvingly when she opened the
door to his knock.

'You look a million dollars!' he declared with casual
extravagance.

Clad in superbly tailored dark blue himself, he looked
even more than that she could have told him, but settled

for a smile and a mock little bow instead. 'Thank you, sir.'

Lounging now in the sitting-room doorway, still in the soiled jeans and T-shirt that she had worn all day, Jill gave a disgusted snort. 'You sound like Darby and Joan!'

'Courtesy becomes all ages,' Ross answered smoothly. 'I thought you might be having a get-together of your own tonight.'

'Well, you thought wrong,' she said, and turned back abruptly into the room.

Claire waited until they were in the car before apologising for her sister's rudeness. 'I think she's suffering from pre-natal baby blues,' she added by way of excuse.

'I'd say she was suffering withdrawal symptoms after spending too much time with Scott,' Ross remarked drily. 'Anyway, we're not going to spend the evening discussing the two of them.'

'Shouldn't you be showing your face at his stag night, though?' Claire ventured. 'I mean, as his only brother...'

'Getting plastered with the motley crew he likes to call his friends isn't my idea of a good night out. In any case, I'm beyond the age limit.'

According to Jill, he was beyond hers too, she thought, though not by her own reckoning. After knowing Ross, younger men would hold little attraction.

They found the Slaters already waiting at the riverside restaurant out near Bakewell. As tall as Ross, but with a shock of blond hair that kept flopping across his forehead, Neil had the brightest and merriest pair of blue eyes that Claire had ever seen on a man. Diane was tall and blond too, her figure statuesque, her humour bubbling.

'The smaller the packaging, the more exclusive the contents,' she commented when Claire made some semi-joking remark about feeling a bit like a sparrow adopted by a trio of eagles. 'Diamonds don't take up a lot of room—as I keep telling this husband of mine.'

'One, maybe not,' he returned equably. 'The number you'd consider worthwhile, I'd need to hire a pantechnicon!'

'Pure exaggeration!' Eyes the colour of old amber winged a provocative glance at Ross, who was listening to the exchange with easy tolerance. '*You* wouldn't begrudge a girl a few sparklers, would you, sweetie?'

'I thought you all preferred to be called women these days,' he said.

'You're generalising again,' she admonished. 'I've told you about that before.' She shook her head resignedly at Claire. 'Deaf as a post when he wants to be, don't you find?'

'I wouldn't know,' Claire answered lightly. 'I haven't tried telling him anything.'

Seeing his mouth take on the familiar slant from the corner of her eye, she could have kicked herself. She felt the warmth rising under her skin, and could do nothing to stop it. Damn him, she thought furiously. Why did he have to be the one man to make her feel this way?

Neil gave her a lazy smile. 'And I get stuck with motor mouth!'

'I'll give you "motor mouth"!' threatened his wife in mock indignation, and he turned the smile on her.

'So what's new?'

Claire had to laugh. They were a double act, each feeding off the other. No malice in it, though. Underneath all the banter, she sensed a very real and very deep regard. She envied them that.

All in all, she enjoyed the evening. Ross could be as blithe as anyone when the mood took him, she discovered.

'It's good to see him let go,' Diane observed when both men were away from the table for a few minutes.

'He's had a lot of extra responsibility thrust on him since his father was taken ill. I think you're going to be good for him.'

Claire shook her head, fingers toying with her glass. 'It isn't like that. I'm only here because he thought it would be nice for me to meet you before the wedding.'

'Oh, really?' The other woman sounded a little non-plussed. 'I could have sworn——' She broke off, shrugging smooth shoulders. 'Shows how perceptive I am. Anyway, I'm glad he did bring you. You're very different from what I imagined.'

'You mean, you thought Jill and I might both be on the make?'

There was a slight pause, then a rueful laugh. 'You don't hold back, do you? Perhaps I did at that. When Ross rang to arrange this, he gave the impression that you and he were...involved in some way, I suppose. I expected some *femme fatale* to walk through the door.'

'The type he usually goes for?'

'Well, like most men, he has been known to tend towards the fancier packaging at times. A low boredom threshold usually takes care of things; beauty and brains aren't always part of the same parcel. You, now, are lovely to look at and bright as a button to boot.' She gave a hoot of laughter. 'How's that for a neat bit of phrasing!'

'Terrific,' Claire said drily, taking it all with a pinch of salt. Attractive she knew she was, but Jill was the beauty.

'Your sister's a very pretty girl,' Diane went on, almost as if she had caught the thought. 'We saw her with Scott in Derby the other day. They neither of them look old enough to be out of school, much less having a baby. Scott's years in university certainly didn't mature him any.' She hesitated a moment before adding diffidently,

'It can't have been easy for you, losing your parents that way. I doubt if I could have coped at all.'

Claire kept her tone easy. 'You would if you'd had to. A case of needs must.'

The men were coming back, threading their way between the tables, the one so dark, the other so fair—both of them drawing feminine attention.

Neil might even have a slight edge, taken feature for feature, Claire thought judiciously, but most women would be drawn to the strength of purpose revealed in the other jawline, the tautness of tanned skin over hard male cheekbone, the eyes that could change from dark to light and every shade in between according to mood. She might fall in love with some other man some day, but it wouldn't be in quite the same way. Ross was a once-in-a-lifetime event.

They left the restaurant at eleven, parting in the car park.

'We're planning a barbecue on Sunday, if the weather holds,' said Diane. 'Why don't the two of you come and join us? Nothing elaborate, just a few friends.'

'We planned to go walking,' answered Ross before Claire could say anything. 'We got drenched on Kinder last week, so we'll hopefully have better luck this. Thanks, anyway.'

'You're a foot-slogger too, Claire?' Neil made it sound as if walking for pleasure was way outside his understanding. 'Ye gads and little fishes!'

'Ignore him,' Diane advised. Expression frankly speculative, she added, 'Have a good day, whatever. We'll see you on Thursday.'

'You didn't need to make up an excuse,' Claire said levelly as she walked with Ross to the car. 'If you'd given me the chance, I'd have done it myself.'

'So I might have been a bit premature,' he returned. 'For "planned" substitute "hoped". I thought we might tackle Bleaklow.'

'Are you serious?' she asked uncertainly.

He unlocked the front passenger door, looking down at her with lifted brows. 'Any reason why I shouldn't be? We discovered a shared enthusiasm last week. Why not continue to share it? If nothing else, I'll know you're not wandering the countryside on your own.'

She should confess about the rambling group, she told herself, but couldn't bring herself to do it. He might consider that she had made a fool of him in some way.

'I'm not sure I can manage this Sunday, anyway,' she prevaricated.

'Why not?' he insisted. 'You need the break after a week shut up in the shop.'

'I still have to finish Jill's wedding-outfit.' It was an outright lie, but the only thing she could come up with. 'There's no other time.'

Whether he believed it or not, he accepted the excuse without further argument. 'Fair enough. Maybe later then.'

He opened the door for her, saw her into the seat, then went round to slide in himself and start the engine. Claire felt utterly depressed, but knew that she had done the right thing. The more she saw of him, the worse it would be. If he had any inkling at all of how she really felt about him—and he had to have some by now—then he must surely realise himself that she was right. Friendship just wasn't enough.

The drive back to town was accomplished in near silence. They had breasted the final hill and were coasting down towards the spread of lights when Ross pulled in suddenly, where the road curved into a lay-by, and drew to a stop.

'This isn't going to work,' he said flatly. 'I've spent the whole evening watching you across that damned table—remembering the way you looked on Sunday night lying on my bed, waiting for me. I've spent the last three days trying to put you out of mind, and not succeeding. If you still feel the way you did before that dammed phone call came through, then say it now and we'll start over.'

He wasn't saying that he was in love with her, Claire warned herself, struggling to contain the swift surging response, only that he wanted her still. If she went along, and allowed the relationship to develop the way she knew it would, she could well be laying herself open to even deeper eventual heartache.

On the other hand his feelings were hardly likely to evolve beyond physical attraction if she continued to keep him at arm's length, came the immediate rider. If she went through life refusing to take chances for fear of getting hurt, she was going to finish up an embittered old maid.

He was a dark silhouette against the sky, hands still resting on the wheel, face shadowed as he turned his head to look at her.

'So?' he asked. 'At least say *something*!'

Closing out the doubts, Claire brought up both hands and cupped them about the lean jaw, bringing his head down to put her lips to his. His arms came readily about her, drawing her closer, his hands warm at her back. His mouth was tender, passion held in check, but she could sense the deep-down fire in him. She wanted to stoke that fire, to feel him vibrate with desire the way he had done the other night, to have him make love to her in the very fullest sense. Life was for living, she had told herself not so long ago, so why not start living it?

The buttons of his silk shirt gave easily. She ran her fingers through the hair beneath, loving the crisp, wiry feel of it. Ross caught her hand and lifted it to his lips, kissing her fingertips.

'You're a regular bundle of surprises,' he growled softly.

'I'm fed up of being Miss Goody Two Shoes!' she declared, throwing caution entirely to the winds.

'Goody Two Shoes never had a temper like yours. Come to think of it, I don't know of anyone with a temper to match yours.' He was smiling as he said it. 'Small and fiery, yet totally unpredictable too. I've a feeling you might turn out to be more than I can handle.'

Claire had a feeling that she might turn out to be more than *she* could handle. The elation bubbling up in her was like nothing she had ever experienced before. She met him more than halfway when he kissed her, hungry for all that she had been missing during these last years. Love was wonderful, exhilarating, everything she had imagined. She took his hand and put it on her breast, tremoring as he cupped it to the shape of her. Desire grew in her, turning her insides liquid, her limbs weak.

It was Ross himself who called a halt, looking down at her with a wry twist to his lips. 'I've a suspicion this might be mostly the wine speaking. You had four glasses.'

Had she? Claire couldn't remember. Not that she gave a damn anyway right now. She had never felt so sexy, so daring, so utterly and deliciously spontaneous. If this were Sunday night all over again, there would be no hesitation, no matter who telephoned!

Ross kissed her once more, then put her firmly from him. 'I'm taking you home to sleep it off,' he declared. 'There's always another day.'

Claire didn't want to go, but he was giving her no choice. She put her head back against the rest as he fired the engine and moved out from the lay-by, consoling herself with the thought of other times to come. From now on she was going to make the most of each and

every moment that the two of them spent together, regardless of what might or might not happen. If it was
meant to be, it would be.

The euphoria had begun to fade a little by the time
they reached the house. Enough so for relief to take precedence over disappointed when Ross elected not to come
in.

'How about tomorrow?' he said at the door. 'I'll pick
you up from the shop.'

And take her where? she wondered, sobered enough
now to know doubt again. Whatever his intentions, they
didn't have to include any long-term commitment. Was
she really ready to embark on an affair that might come
to nothing in the end?

'I'm not sure,' she said. 'The dress——'

'You've all day Sunday to finish that,' he returned
firmly. 'Don't start playing fast and loose with me again.
Either you want to see me or you don't. Which?'

Green eyes took on a spark. 'Jill said you were bossy!'

'Jill doesn't know the half of it.' He was smiling, but
adamant still. 'Are you going to make up your mind,
or do I do it for you?'

'How?' she challenged, and stifled an involuntary yelp
as he hoisted her up on her toes to reach her mouth with
his. The kiss was long, lingering and wholly will-sapping.
Claire let herself go with it, relishing the feel of him
hardening against her.

'Will you stay the same for two damned consecutive
minutes!' he groaned when she slipped from his grasp
at last. 'You've got me spinning like a top!'

The way to keep him coming, she thought on a re-
surgence of reckless abandon. 'Six o'clock sharp,' she
said. 'Goodnight, sweet prince!'

She slid quickly inside and closed the door on him,
standing there with her back to it, listening to his laugh.

'You,' he said softly but plainly, 'are going to pay for that.'

Perhaps in more ways than one, she reflected, but refused to let it deter her.

She listened to the fading engine sound, contemplating the climb upstairs and preparation for her lonely bed without enthusiasm.

Coming out from the sitting-room, Jill regarded her with jaundiced expression.

'I hope you realise you're just the latest in a long line,' she said.

Not necessarily so, thought Claire resolutely, turning to slide the bolt. Who was to say that, given time and incentive, Ross might not come to feel for her as she felt for him? Wanting her the way he did was at least a start.

Saturday was one of the best days she had had so far. The customer flow seemed never-ending. At times like this she could do with an assistant, Claire admitted, trying to do several things at the same time. Perhaps, if the bank came through, she could at least get someone in on a Saturday. The problem was that it really needed to be someone with experience in ladies' outfitting, and he or she was unlikely to come cheap.

At a quarter to six, reckoning on no further custom, she closed shop and took advantage of the respite to have a quick wash in the little cloakroom backing off the office, and to change her grey suit for an emerald dress with a scooped neckline and softly pleated skirt. Green was a bit obvious with her hair and eyes, she supposed, but it suited her.

Her hand felt far from steady as she applied lipstick. Had anyone told her two short weeks ago that she would find herself in this position, she would have laughed in their face. Falling in love with Ross had been the furthest thought from her mind.

By half-past six, with still no sign of him, she was torn between concern that something might have happened to him and the increasing suspicion that he might have thought better of the whole affair after all. If the latter, he could at least have let her know, she fumed, taking refuge in anger.

At six-forty she gave up hope altogether and set off for home. She had come in on the bus that morning owing to the arrangement. She took a taxi back, damning the expense. The way she felt, even the shop took second place.

Jill was out, whether with Scott or not there was no way of telling. Wherever she was, it was to be hoped that her mood had improved, thought Claire wearily. She only wished that the wedding itself was over and done with.

She made herself a mug of coffee, but wanted nothing to eat. Her heart leapt when the phone rang, but it was only one of her hiking friends wanting to know if she would be going tomorrow. She should say yes, she knew. Moping around the house was no way to carry on. On the other hand, the garden needed attention.

'Other things to do, I'm afraid,' she told him. 'Maybe next week.'

Going up to her bedroom, she took off the emerald dress and put on her nightdress and négligé, intending to watch a little television and then go to bed as soon as it was dark—a lousy way to spend Saturday night, only what else was there?

The smooth coolness of satin next to her skin was something of a comfort. Much of her apparently expensive underwear and nightwear was bought from a seconds shop, and so wasn't all that extravagant, but even this minor luxury might have to go eventually if the present little boom in business failed to last. A bit of a waste, anyway, she supposed, with no one but herself to see it. Cotton was far more practical.

The summer TV schedules aroused little enough interest. The one film she hadn't already seen was so slow that it put her to sleep. The doorbell woke her some ten minutes or so later. Jill's forgotten her key again, she thought hazily, struggling up from the depths.

Expecting to see her sister on the doorstep, she went to open up, and gazed in some confusion at the man standing there.

'Sorry about the delay,' Ross apologised. 'I was stuck in a traffic jam on the M1 for over two hours. An articulated lorry overturned and blocked all three lanes. I tried phoning you, but couldn't get through.'

Where, Claire found time to wonder, had he been coming from on the M1? It was a question which was swiftly swamped beneath a tide of relief at the realisation that he hadn't, after all, let her down purposely.

'You'll not have eaten, then?' she said, stepping back to allow him entry.

'Not since lunch,' he acknowledged. He ran an eye over her, brows lifting quizzically. 'Oh, ye of little faith!'

'How was I to know what had happened?' she defended.

'I'd have expected you to take it for granted that I wouldn't just opt out on an arrangement.'

'I hardly know you well enough to be that sure.'

The grey eyes acquired a deeper hue. 'Then we'd better take steps to rectify the matter.'

The kiss left her breathless and aching for more of the same. It took a real effort to laugh and say lightly '*That* wasn't quite the way I meant!'

'It's a starting point,' he said, equally lightly. 'In the meantime, we have a choice. You can either get dressed again and we'll go out to dinner, or we can fix ourselves something right here—always assuming you haven't eaten already, that is.'

Claire knew which she preferred. Heart lilting, she shook her head. 'To answer the last first—no, I haven't. As to the other... it's a bit late to start thinking about going out now. There's some cold chicken in the fridge, and plenty of salad. Not a lot to offer a hungry man. I know, but——'

'But sufficient to keep body and soul together.' Ross turned her about, dropping a light kiss on the top of her head. 'I like the outfit,' he added softly.

Rather more concealing than the shirt he had provided, she thought, unaware of the way in which the ivory satin moulded itself lovingly to every slender curve as she moved ahead of him. There was little point in getting dressed again, anyway.

'I'm afraid I can't offer you any really decent wine,' she said, trying not to sound over-apologetic about it. 'I doubt if you'd think much of supermarket plonk.'

'Not necessarily so,' he responded, 'but I'd as soon just settle for the chicken.'

Claire was in total agreement. She wanted no wine fumes clouding her judgement tonight. It would be all too easy to give way to the hunger he so swiftly and effortlessly aroused in her. Too easy, and too meaningless as yet. If they made love at all, it had to be more than just a physical thing for them both.

They ate in the kitchen, taking coffee through to the sitting-room afterwards. Seated beside Ross on the sofa, Claire was reminded forcefully of the last time she had made coffee for him. The tempers had been short that night, the words harsh, yet, if Ross was to be believed, the attraction had been there for him even then.

'Do you still feel the same way about the wedding?' she asked on impulse.

'I still have the same doubts about what comes after, if that's what you mean,' he said. 'They've neither of them given me any reason to change my views.'

Claire looked at him with faintly drawn brows. 'You don't hate Scott, do you?'

'Of course not. I have the same feelings for him that you have for Jill. That doesn't mean I can't criticise him when it's merited.'

'Has he always been a bit ... self-centred?'

'Over-indulged children do tend that way. He came along when my mother had more or less given up hope of having another. Forty was thought to be over the hill for child-bearing twenty years ago. He was premature too, which didn't help. Mollycoddled from the word go, you might say.'

'Were you jealous of all the attention he was given?'

Grey eyes crinkled at the corners. 'At twelve, I was a mite past either wanting or needing all that much attention myself. If going away to school does nothing else it instils independence. It would have done Scott a lot of good.'

Claire wasn't sure about that, but wasn't about to enter into another argument on the subject either. She caught a fleeting glimpse of her reflection in the mirror on the wall opposite as she reached for her coffee-cup, her hair lit by the glow from the electric log fire in the hearth, her skin warm-toned within the crossed V of her wrap. Her sitting here in her night-things had to be considered somewhat provocative, yet Ross showed no sign of being overcome by desire.

Hands linked comfortably behind his head, legs stretched, he looked thoroughly relaxed. He was dressed casually in fawn trousers and lightweight white sweater, so he obviously hadn't intended taking her anywhere too up-market. It was even possible that he'd planned on going straight to the flat from the shop.

The firmly chiselled lines of his mouth were a turn-on all on their own. Her own lips tingled at the memory of his kiss out in the hall. She had never wanted anything as much as she wanted him. Not just physically, but all the way through.

'If you don't stop looking at me like that,' he said, almost conversationally, 'I'm going to lose hold of my better intentions.'

Her voice came out husky. 'Better than what?'

'Than rushing you into something you're not ready for.' He swivelled his head to look at her, smile wry. 'Patience was never one of my virtues, as you probably already gathered. Seeing you in that shirt of mine last week was more than flesh and blood could stand.'

'It takes two,' Claire murmured. 'I wasn't exactly unwilling.' She searched the lean features, trying not to read too much into too little. 'You called me unpredictable last night, but you're even more so.'

'Only because you've seen me purely as a libertine up to now.' The smile grew as he registered the expression in her eyes. 'Men who reach my age without having acquired themselves a wife often find themselves labelled as womanisers.'

'Only where there's been enough of a turnover to merit it,' she said, not about to take that at face value. 'You do have something of a reputation.'

'Reputations are built as much on hearsay as actual performance. You'll have to take that on trust.'

The whole tenor of the conversation seemed to be leading somewhere, though Claire still wasn't sure just where that might be. She studied him from beneath her lashes, eliciting a change of expression on his part, and a smothered groan.

'Will you stop doing that? I'm having a hard enough job keeping my hands off you as it is!'

'So why try?' she asked recklessly, abandoning restraint. 'If it's what we both want...'

Ross made no immediate move, just reclined there, gazing at her meditatively. 'What *I* want,' he said at length, 'is to change your whole opinion of me. We had a bad start. Mostly down to my tactics, I admit. I tackled the whole thing the wrong way. Finding myself instantly attracted to you was no great help when I'd already convinced myself that you were probably no better than your sister.

'And no, I don't see her as a promiscuous little tart any more,' he added as she opened her mouth to protest. 'In need of a short, sharp shock or two, maybe, but no more than many others her age. The pity of it is that Scott is hardly a stabilising influence.'

'Marriage and parenthood might settle them both down,' suggested Claire, without too much hope. 'In any case, it's out of our hands.'

'And not a subject I intended getting into tonight.' His gaze moved from her face down the length of her throat to the creamy swell where the satin material had fallen slightly aside; a muscle tensed visibly in his jaw. 'To hell with it,' he said roughly, and reached for her.

Claire went to him only too willingly, returning his kisses without reserve. Whatever his long-term intentions might be, she was going to make the most of the here and now, she told herself.

CHAPTER TEN

STILL kissing her, Ross untied the belt of her wrap and slid it from her shoulders. Claire allowed the wide sleeves to fall, lifting her arms free to slide them about his neck and abandon herself even further to the gathering tumult. She was nude beneath the thin layer of satin, her skin sensitised to every movement. The feel of those long lean fingers slowly and delicately traversing her spinal column from her nape down to the point where it vanished beneath the low-cut back of her nightdress was a sensual revelation.

'Fragile as a Ming vase,' he murmured against her temple. 'Have you any idea how utterly appealing that makes you?'

'I always thought men preferred taller women,' she murmured back, too lost in the delight of it all to resent the fragility label.

He laughed low down in his throat. 'I thought I did too, until I met you and came over all protective.'

'It wasn't noticeable.'

'Initially, maybe not. I was too intent on covering up the impact you'd made. Finding you on your own on Kinder brought it home to me. You won't like me saying it, but someone your size has to be even more at risk.' He paused, looking down at her with a suddenly serious expression. 'Promise me you won't attempt to go it alone again.'

Now was the time to tell him the truth, she knew, but she found herself rather liking the solicitude. 'I promise,' she said, and saw the seriousness give way to slightly ironical humour.

'A little too quick and ready for total conviction, but I'll give you the benefit of the doubt.'

His regard heated again as he registered the shimmer in her eyes. He smoothed a hand over the tumbled copper hair and down her cheek, following the tender line of her jaw. Claire felt the tremors start deep inside as he moved on to slide one thin strap from her shoulder. Her breast looked so small in his palm, the nipple a mere rosy bud. Virginal was the word that sprang to mind; she wondered if the fact that she was one still was part of her continuing attraction for him.

The touch of his lips was like fire and ice at one and the same time, dragging a shuddering little cry from her lips. She arched her back involuntarily to bring herself into closer proximity, her every sense tuned to the potent caress. The sudden desperate need to touch him in some more intimate way sent her hands searching beneath the thin sweater, fingers curling into the hair on his chest.

His skin was warm and slicked with moisture, his heartbeats quickening at her touch. She could feel his rib-cage beneath the muscle, expanding in tune with his roughened breathing, the musky male odour of his arousal stimulating her to a degree where pure instinct took over.

Ross drew in a harsh breath as her seeking fingers found the catch of his waistband. 'If you do that,' he said roughly, 'there'll be no stopping. It took too much out of me last time.'

This time she would ignore the phone if it rang was Claire's first thought, followed immediately by the realisation that a phone call was probably the least likely interruption. For Jill to walk in on them would be disastrous.

'I think I'd better leave,' he added with obvious reluctance as she stayed her movements. 'I didn't intend to go even this far tonight. Not with those two likely to put in an appearance any time.' Eyes rueful, he kissed the end of her nose, then pulled up her nightdress to cover her breast, sliding the strap back over her shoulder. 'So much for strength of mind!'

He was showing more of it now than she felt capable of producing, Claire acknowledged, Jill or no Jill. She didn't want him to go—couldn't bear the thought of being left on her own with all the turmoil going on inside her still.

'Pity about tomorrow,' he observed, getting to his feet with an apparent recovery rate which she envied. 'The forecast is good.'

It was on the tip of her tongue to tell him the truth about that too, but it smacked of too much eagerness. Let him set the pace. That way she ran no risk of betraying herself.

'Diane rang this morning to ask me to bring you over for dinner at their place Tuesday night,' he added, as if in sudden recollection. 'How are you fixed?'

She kept her tone light. 'I'm not doing anything else.'

'Good.' Ross drew her upright, holding her there in front of him to plant a brief, unsatisfying kiss on her mouth. 'I'll pick you up around half-past seven.'

'If you give me the address, I can drive over myself,' she said. 'Save you having to bring me all the way back here afterwards.'

'If you're thinking I might make a late-night detour by my place, the ball will be entirely in your court,' he responded with irony.

If that was true, there was a good chance of him winning game, set *and* match, she thought.

She saw him to the door, finding time to wonder what he might be doing and who he might be seeing on Monday evening. He kissed her again before departing, leaving her yearning for more. A man worth going out on a limb for, she thought, watching him cross to the car before finally closing the door. Whether she would feel the same in time to come she neither knew nor cared at present.

Jill still wasn't home when she went upstairs at eleven. Her bed wasn't even made, Claire noted on passing the open door of her room. She went in to straighten the rumpled duvet and plump up the pillows, wondering if Scott was any tidier in his habits. Not that they'd either of them probably need to be while they were living at the Laxton homestead, with Alice around to take care of things.

It was when she went to tidy the equally messy dressing-table that she saw the opened box of tampons. Even then, realisation didn't dawn for several seconds.

There were two tampons missing. Gazing at the rest, Claire sank down slowly on to the dressing-stool, reluctant to take in the implications.

What seemed clear was the fact that if there had ever been a pregnancy there almost certainly wasn't any more. A mistake after all, perhaps? Except that the gynaecologist could hardly have confirmed a non-existent condition.

Which left ... what? Jill might have been a little out of sorts this past day or two, but miscarriages surely caused far more distress than she had shown.

The only remaining explanation was one Claire could hardly bear to consider. If it was true, then Scott had to be in on it too. Not that that made things any better.

She was still sitting there when she heard the car draw up outside some minutes later. There were footsteps on the gravel, a muffled giggle followed by the scrape of a key in the latch, another giggle, inside this time, and the faint creak of the sitting-room door being opened as the front one was closed. That meant Scott was staying a while.

Meeting her own darkened gaze in the mirror, Claire felt numbness give way to white-hot anger. The time to tackle the two of them was right now, together, with the evidence to hand. She was making no mistake. There had never been a baby!

The sitting-room was in darkness, the door left partly ajar. Claire reached in a hand and switched on the overhead light, startling the couple on the sofa into jerky movement apart.

'I thought you were in bed,' said Jill, sounding more accusatory than apologetic.

Unabashed, Scott eyed the satin ensemble with an approval too reminiscent of his brother's response. 'You'd have knocked any burglars for six in that,' he commented.

Claire ignored the sally, intent only on the anger and hurt boiling up in her.

'I found these on your dressing-table,' she clipped. tossing the box she was holding to Jill, who caught it instinctively. 'Perhaps you might like to tell me the real story, not the fabricated one!'

For the very first time since she had known him, Scott looked discomfited. More resignation than guilt, even so, Claire reckoned. Jill at least had the grace to flush.

'You shouldn't have been in my room,' she muttered. 'I thought I'd left the light on myself.'

'Considering it must still have been light when you went out, it was hardly likely. I went in to——' Claire caught herself up, shaking her head impatiently. 'That's irrelevant, anyway. Liars should be more careful of what evidence they leave lying around. You never *were* pregnant, were you? You put everyone through all this for nothing!'

'Not for nothing.' Scott was sitting up straight, his handsome features set in lines that made him look older than his age for once. 'It was the best way of making sure none of you put too big a spoke in the wheel.'

'We knew nobody would want us to get married,' said Jill, rallying her forces. 'You and Ross alone would have done everything you could to stop it! We could have gone off on our own and done it. How would you have felt about that?'

'Probably a great deal better than I feel about this!' Claire retorted. 'At the very least, it wouldn't have been quite as much strain on Scott's father. As to our stopping you, how could we? No matter what we thought about it, you're both of age—in years, if not in the head!'

'You don't know my brother,' Scott cut in darkly. 'He'd have found a way. He was bad enough before he took over the company—pushing me around. He thinks he's lord of the whole blasted manor now!'

'If trying to get you to accept a little responsibility is what we're talking about, I'd say he has every reason to come the heavy,' she returned scathingly. 'I'd doubt if you've even been near the office since all this started.'

'You'd be right too. I'm just a dogsbody—not even on the board. I've as much right as he has to be there!'

'Because you're family, you mean? How about basic interest in the firm, dedication to putting in a good day's work, ability to make decisions—all the little things directors are usually required to show? The way you see things, you'd hardly be an asset.'

More blue than grey, Scott's eyes were blazing, his whole face rigid. 'What would *you* know about it? You and your tinpot little shop! What would you know about anything! You might think you've got Ross taped, but don't count on it. Don't count on anything where he's concerned. He'll dump you the same way he's dumped all the others, as soon as he's had what he's after.'

'Scott, don't!' For the first time, Jill sounded genuinely distressed. 'It isn't a tinpot little shop. Claire's worked long and hard to keep us both going all these years.'

Whatever hurt had been caused by Scott's caustic comments, Claire found her sister's defence uplifting. 'It doesn't matter,' she assured her, on a slightly softer note.

'Yes, it does.' Scott's whole demeanour had undergone a change—he looked almost ashamed. 'Jill's right, I shouldn't have said any of that, but you're not the only one with a temper. I've taken enough stick from Ross without hearing it from you too. You don't know what it's been like having him held up as an example all my life!'

'No, I don't,' Claire agreed, taking the last with a pinch of salt. 'In any case, it's hardly the main issue.'

Two pairs of eyes regarded her with near-identical expressions, but it was left to Scott to put it into words. 'The wedding is going ahead, come what may. If you don't want to upset my father even more, you'll let things lie.'

Claire put out a hand to the doorjamb, legs too unsteady to support her unaided any longer. 'It has to come out some time.'

'So we'll cross that bridge later.'

'Your mother's having a nursery prepared,' she reminded him, still hardly able to believe that he could be so cavalier about it all.

'Not right away. There'll be plenty of time. Jill might even have a miscarriage on honeymoon. That would save a whole lot of trouble.'

'Please, Claire.' Jill was pleading now. 'I know we've gone about things in a rotten way, but you have to admit you'd have done anything to stop us getting married otherwise.'

'I'd have put up whatever arguments against it that I could find, yes,' Claire was bound to agree. 'But, as I keep telling you, in the long run I couldn't have stopped you. Neither could anyone on your side,' she added to Scott. 'What really hurts is that there was no real need for any of this. All both of you had to do was hold out against pressure.'

Scott lifted his shoulders. 'Too late now—it's done. The question is, are you going to keep quiet about it?'

'I don't have very much choice, do I?' she said unhappily. 'Your father seems to have taken things fairly well so far. Finding out it was all a lie might just tip the balance. We'll just have to hope he'll be able to take the so-called miscarriage without suffering any repercussions.'

'He's on limited time, anyway, according to the specialists,' came the unemotional comment, drawing a fresh surge of anger from her.

'Don't be so bloody callous!'

'I'm not.' He seemed more surprised by the invective than defensive about what he had said. 'I'm just stating a fact. It doesn't mean I've no feeling for him.'

Whatever feeling he did have, it certainly lacked the kind of depth which one would normally associate with a son for his father, Claire judged. Whether his feelings for Jill went all that much deeper was open to speculation too—something else to worry about.

'It might be a good idea if you went home,' she said. 'I'd like to talk to Jill on her own.'

'You'll not talk her out of it,' he declared with conviction.

'I'm not going to try.'

'You go, Scott,' said Jill. 'I'll see you tomorrow.'

He hesitated a moment longer before getting reluctantly to his feet, pulling her up with him to kiss her with an air of defiance Claire would have found amusing under other circumstances. They were just two kids intent on having their own way, she reflected. Odd to think that she was only two years older than Scott herself.

She stepped aside to allow him to pass, but made no attempt to sit down, despite the unsteadiness still in her knees. Jill went with him to the door, coming back to stand in the sitting-room doorway much as Claire had done, face reflecting the same defiant expression.

'I really don't see any point in discussing it any further,' she said. 'I'm sorry for lying to you, but, as

Scott said, it's done now so what's the use? Providing
you keep it to yourself, no one else need know.'

'You've put me in a lousy position,' Claire pointed
out. 'How do you think I'm going to feel if the Laxtons
mention the baby?'

'If you hadn't gone rooting about in my room, you
wouldn't have known about it. You'll just have to forget
you do know, that's all.' Jill hesitated a moment, as if
in anticipation of some response, looking relieved when
it failed to materialise. 'I'll get to bed, then.'

Left alone, Claire made some attempt to come to terms
with the situation. One of the most difficult things was
going to be keeping Ross from suspecting something
wrong. He was too perceptive by half. There wasn't, she
supposed, an awful lot that he could actually do if he
did discover the truth, but she didn't want to be the one
to let it out. Her ability to dissemble was going to be
tested to the limit.

She spent Sunday on the garden. Scott came for Jill
around eleven. They didn't say where they were going,
and Claire didn't care to ask. In a few days, Jill would
be gone from the house altogether, so she might as well
get used to it, she told herself.

She might even put the house on the market and take
a flat closer to town. Jill would be entitled to half of
anything left over, of course. She was ethically entitled
to half the business too, if it came to that, considering
that the money to start it had come from their parents.

It was doubtful if she would ever claim her share,
Claire deliberated, leaning on the lawn-mower, but the
possibility had to be faced. Scott might have future
financial problems, or even find that his present income
didn't stretch quite far enough to support two in the
manner to which he was accustomed and Jill fast becoming so.

Whichever, there was no use worrying about it now, she came to the conclusion. She had more than enough on her plate already.

By Tuesday's closing time she had reached a state of mind where little seemed worth worrying about any more. What would happen, would happen regardless, so she would simply take it as it came, she decided. If that turned out to include Ross too, then so be it.

She dressed for the evening with extra care from the skin outwards, donning delicate lacy underwear and gossamer-fine stockings before slipping into the classic black dress she had brought home with her from stock. The opera top left her shoulders bare; the straight-cut skirt outlined her hips.

Viewing herself in the mirror, she knew a momentary doubt, quickly brushed aside. The last thing she intended thinking about tonight was Jill and Scott's deception. They weren't around, thank heaven.

Ross looked devastating, as always, in silver-grey. He wore clothes so well, Claire reflected in the car. He looked pretty wonderful out of them too, if it came to that. She could visualise him now in her mind's eye—so fit, so strong, so vital! Her pulses were leaping all over the place at the very memory.

The Slater home was only a couple of miles away from the Laxtons', and almost as imposing. Diane was wearing black too, which fined down her voluptuous figure.

'Two minds with but a single thought!' she greeted Claire cheerfully. 'I wish I could wear that style of neckline. I tend to spill out of anything too low-cut.'

'Quantity *and* quality in your case,' said Ross, eyeing her cleavage with mock-lasciviousness. 'You were always well-endowed, even as a schoolgirl!'

'You mean downright fat,' she derided, and he grinned.

'Depends on the viewpoint.'

Claire kept a smile on her face with difficulty. If he liked big breasts so much, what did he see in her? she wondered.

Neil took her through to the drawing-room to introduce her to the other four guests already gathered there. She hadn't realised there were to be any others, and was unprepared for the interest her relationship with Ross appeared to be eliciting.

'It's surprising to find the two of you on such good terms considering the way things are,' commented one of the women, with what Claire considered a distinct lack of tact and diplomacy.

'Let not the siblings take issue,' said Ross lightly, coming up in time to catch the last remark. 'You're looking very smart tonight, Pauline. Red is definitely your colour.'

The compliment brought a sudden sparkle to eyes that a moment before had been tinged with something approaching hostility. 'I've been told that before.'

And by Ross himself, if she read the signals correctly, thought Claire. One of his exes, no doubt.

Tall and dark himself, though lacking the charisma which Ross emanated so effortlessly, the other woman's husband looked on with a resigned expression. Second-best, and aware of it, Claire judged.

She found herself seated next to him at table. His name was Miles as she already knew. He was in computers he told her, when she asked the nature of his business. 'Who isn't these days?' he quipped self-deprecatingly.

Claire laughed. 'Well, I'm not for one. I haven't so much as touched a computer in years.'

'You'd find one very helpful in your business affairs,' he said. 'Accounts instantly to hand at a keystroke.'

'Gone forever, at another!' She shook her head. 'I can handle a typewriter far better than I ever could a computer, out-dated though it might be.'

A burst of laughter drew her attention across the wide table. Ross had Diane on one side and Pauline on the other, and seemed equally at ease with both. The three of them were sharing the joke, whatever it was, with Diane in imminent danger of baring a boob regardless as her chest heaved with merriment.

'Some men can attract women without even trying,' commented Miles with just a hint of acridity. 'I hope you're not the jealous type.'

Claire kept her tone light. 'I've never had reason to be.'

'No, well, with your looks, I don't suppose you'd have to be.'

A heavy-handed compliment at best, she thought drily, summoning a smile and a murmured thanks. Catching Ross's eye as he glanced in her direction, she kept the smile on her lips, and was rewarded by the slow widening of his own. Jealous she refused to be, no matter how much attention he paid to the other women. He was a free agent.

The party adjourned to the terrace for coffee and liqueurs. It was a sultry evening, with thunder rumbling in the far distance from time to time. Diane lit aromatic candles to keep any flying stock away, and these cast flickering shadows over the gathered faces.

'Candlelight is so much more romantic, don't you think?' she said to no one in particular. 'I'd love to have lived in a pre-electric age.'

'Minus dishwasher, hair-drier, microwave, stereo, and all the rest you can't live without now,' snorted Neil.

'What you've never had you can't miss,' came the unruffled response. 'I'd rather fancy myself in a crinoline.'

'Along with half the male population,' said Ross, drawing a provocative glance.

'I do nothing by halves, darling.'

Claire joined in the general laughter. Diane's flirtatiousness was pure pantomime. She really liked her, much more so than the scarlet-clad brunette still discharging the occasional ''he was mine before he was yours'' message.

Ross was sitting on the arm of her chair, his own arm resting along the back. On impulse, she let her head go back a little until her nape came into contact with his sleeve, seeing the sudden contraction about Pauline's mouth with a sense of satisfaction. Put that in your pipe and smoke it! she thought.

She felt Ross glance down at her, but wasn't ready for the hand that descended on to her shoulder, the light caress of his fingers against the side of her neck in passing—a proprietorial gesture that drew every eye and set her pulses humming. It took everything she had to retain at least an external composure.

The thunder was closer now, preceded by flashes of lightning that made night into day every few minutes.

'It's going to be a real humdinger when it finally gets here,' said Neil as the wind began to rise. 'What say we retire indoors before the rain comes?'

With a spot or two already felt, no one was going to disagree. They slung covers over the chairs just in time as the heavens opened.

Had she been on her own, Claire would have sat through the following hour or so biting her nails. She had hated thunderstorms since the night of her eighth birthday, when lightning had struck the television aerial, blowing out the front of the set. No one had been injured, but the incident had left its mark.

The safest place to be, she had read somewhere, was in a car, grounded by four big rubber tyres. She had even on occasion gone and sat a storm out in the Panda, although she still hadn't felt wholly convinced.

Now, seeing the way the rest of the party totally ignored the noise, she felt ashamed of her fears. She did her best to stop herself from jumping out of her skin every time the thunder cracked, trying to concentrate on the general conversation. Sitting at her side, Ross must have been aware of the tension in her, but he made no comment, much to her relief.

It was gone midnight before the storm finally passed over, though the rain continued to pour down. Miles was the first to suggest leaving, pleading an early appointment.

'We'd better be going too,' said Ross. 'Long drive.' He stood up, offering a hand to Claire, his smile a stimulant in itself. 'Ready?'

For a whimsical moment, she wondered what his reaction would be if she said no. Not that she had any such intention. With the shop due to open at nine sharp, it was going to be a short enough night as it was.

'See you both on Thursday, then,' said Diane at the door. 'Always providing the bride and groom don't decide to elope at the last minute.'

It was something of a shock for Claire to realise that she hadn't even thought about the new development during the last few hours. Elopement at the outset would have saved a whole lot of trouble in the long run, she thought wryly.

She was quiet in the car—enough so to draw a quizzical glance from Ross.

'Tired?'

What he was really asking was if she wanted to be taken straight back home, Claire reckoned, and she acknowledged there and then that it simply wasn't in her to keep on holding out against the need that had been building in her all day. Whatever the future had in store, she was going to have tonight to remember.

'Not *too* tired,' she said with delicate emphasis.

CHAPTER ELEVEN

Ross made no immediate comment, though Claire doubted if he had mistaken her meaning. She stole a glance at the clean-cut profile, wishing she could tell what he was really thinking, how he really felt.

'You sure about this?' he asked at length, jerking her pulses.

'Never more so,' she assured him resolutely. 'I want you, Ross.'

His mouth slanted. 'Hold that thought. We still have some way to go.'

Too far, she reflected, watching the headlights cutting a swathe through the dark, empty road ahead—another twenty minutes at least before they reached the flat. She was going to be tired in the morning, but she didn't care. This was more important to her than anything else right now.

Ross made no attempt to switch on any lights when they reached the flat; he just took her in his arms and kissed her into a state where she scarcely knew what day it was, before taking her hand and leading her through to the bedroom. Claire felt no qualms as he slowly but surely undressed her, only the same overwhelming need.

When he came to her at last, nude as she was herself, she could hardly contain her emotions, kissing him in a fervour of desire, loving the strength of him, the lean muscularity rippling beneath her hands, the sheer masculine dominance of his lovemaking. Ready though he undoubtedly was, he didn't rush her, but used both hands and lips to elicit a degree of pleasure that she hadn't

imagined existed, murmuring words of endearment that
swelled her heart to bursting point.

She opened to him like a flower, moist and welcoming
when the moment finally came. The initial pain lasted
bare seconds, followed by a flooding exultancy as he slid
all the way inside her.

Whatever she had imagined the sensation to be, it came
nowhere near this wonderful, consummate merging of
flesh with flesh, this sense of belonging, of having found
the one man in the world who was meant for her. She
moved in tune with the long slow thrusts, wordless cries
torn from her throat as the pace quickened, carrying the
two of them on to a shattering, earth-shaking climax.

Ross was the first to stir, lifting his head to look down
into her face with eyes more tender than she had ever
seen them.

'You,' he said softly, 'are a revelation! The thought
of anyone else——' He broke off, shaking his head.
'Ignore that.'

Swamped by emotion, Claire abandoned all pretence.
'I don't want anyone else,' she vowed. 'I'll never want
anyone else!'

It was difficult to read every nuance of expression in
the darkness. 'Never is a long time,' he said on a guarded
note. 'You've only known me a couple of weeks all told—
and for most of that you didn't even like me all that
much.'

'Not true.' She brought up a hand and ran her fingertips over the strong mouth, tremoring anew at the com-
motion even that simple contact aroused in her. 'Not
completely, anyway,' she amended. 'I didn't like the way
you made me feel—especially when you were pulling Jill
to pieces.'

Ross kissed her fingers, his smile faint. 'I'd be a liar
if I claimed to have changed my mind where that young
lady is concerned. Where I *was* wrong was in laying all
the blame at your door. You could hardly be expected

to run the business single-handed and keep full control over a wayward teenager. God knows, I had enough trouble trying to keep Scott on the reasonably straight and narrow.'

He rolled on to his back, drawing her close to lie with her head pillowed on his shoulder, and smoothing her hair with his hand. 'I was fighting something of a battle with myself, if it comes to that. I never expected to find myself being bowled over by the older sister of the girl I was convinced was on the make.'

'You didn't give the impression of being bowled over,' murmured Claire, inhaling the scent of him.

He gave a short laugh. 'If there's one thing I've learned, it's not to give the game away. Women learn young to take advantage of any lever.'

'Not all,' she objected. 'Diane said you were too fond of generalising.'

'Diane isn't beyond a bit of advantage-taking herself on occasion.'

Claire tried to keep her tone light. 'Of you?'

'If you're asking if there's ever been anything between us, the answer is no,' he returned levelly. 'She wasn't the one who rang the other night.' His hand had moved down via her throat to her breast, the caress gently possessive. 'It was just a casual acquaintance. I'm not involved with anyone else.'

The 'else' warmed her. She put her lips to his shoulder, running her hand down over the broad chest to trace the ridged stomach muscle, sliding over hard male hip-bone to find evidence of his revitalisation, enclosing him in her hand with a sense of power as his breathing roughened.

'Can we do it again?' she asked huskily.

'Try and stop me,' he growled.

The first time had been wonderful enough, but the second time was even better. A woman of experience at last, was Claire's fleeting thought as she came slowly back to the surface again. She felt utterly fulfilled.

It was gone two when he finally drove her home. Claire yearned to go back with him, to spend the night wrapped in his arms. If it hadn't been for the shop, she could have stayed. For the very first time she actively resented the commitment.

'I'm entertaining some business connections tomorrow evening,' he said at the door, 'so I shan't see you before the wedding. It's going to be something of a rush for you, isn't it?'

The cars were due at two-twenty—not a lot of time in which to get home after closing the shop at one and get ready, Claire had to agree.

'I'll manage,' she said. 'I'm so glad Mr Johnson agreed to give Jill away. I'd have felt so out of place doing it myself.'

Ross moved a stray strand of copper hair from her face, his touch gentle. 'You wouldn't have been setting any precedents, but I can appreciate the feeling.'

'You should really be best man, though,' she added, reluctant to let him leave. 'Brothers usually are.'

'A role I'd have declined even if asked. He's better off with one of his friends.' He slid a light hand down her cheek, lifting her chin for a goodnight kiss that went little way towards satisfying the hunger still inside her. His smile lit further rockets. 'Sleep tight, Green-eyes.'

The way she felt, it would be a miracle if she slept at all, she thought, wishing she could be as sure of his feelings as she was of her own. For all she knew this was all there was, so far as he was concerned.

She did sleep in the end of course, and woke with reluctance to the alarm at seven. Jill was still in bed as usual when she left the house. Whether she would make some effort to change her habits when she was living in the Laxton home was a question Claire hadn't yet cared to put. She doubted it, anyway. Getting her up in time for school had been difficult enough.

The day went through its phases. Arriving home to find Jill not only in but with a meal ready to be eaten— albeit a simple one—was a pleasant surprise.

'I thought it would be nice to spend my last evening at home with you,' said the younger girl. 'Scott and I will have all the time in the world to be together from tomorrow.' She hesitated before tagging on tentatively, 'Thanks for keeping things to yourself.'

Claire gave a little shrug. 'It wouldn't have done any good. Not at this late stage. What worries me most is how the Laxtons are going to take this miscarriage you're planning on announcing.'

'It might not be necessary. We're not taking precautions.'

'There's something of a limit on the length of a pregnancy,' Claire reminded her. 'Anyway, I'd have thought you'd do better to wait a while before you actually planned on having a baby.'

'Oh, I don't know. We'd kind of got used to the idea.' Jill sounded anything but concerned. 'There are some real cute baby clothes around. I've been looking.'

Claire started to remonstrate then desisted, recognising the futility. Jill would go her own way regardless—as would Scott. It was when one began wanting something the other didn't that the trouble would start.

Lucy came round later. The same age as Jill, and equally immature in outlook, she had been sadly disappointed in her friend's decision not to have any bridesmaids. The less fuss the better, Jill had declared when asked. Privately, Claire believed that it was more a case of preferring to be the sole focus of attention on the day. Lucy was far too pretty to fade into any background.

With everything ready for the morrow, Claire was glad to take advantage of an early night, but still found sleep hard to come by. If she lost Ross now, she would go into a convent, she told herself only half jokingly, missing him in every way possible. The very thought of ever making love with another man was anathema to her.

There were more people in the church than anticipated. Making her way down the aisle alongside Mrs Johnson, who had travelled in with her, Claire felt the cynosure of all eyes on her navy blue and white ensemble. She had gone low-key deliberately, although not to the point of abandoning her high heels.

Ross's wink as he looked across at her was a welcome boost to her flagging self-confidence. She winked back, aware of his mother's eyes on the pair of them and suddenly not caring a jot.

The men were wearing lounge suits rather than the morning suits that would probably have been *de rigueur* under normal circumstances. Even without the lie, it was doubtful if the full pomp and circumstance would have been brought into play, Claire reflected. The marriage itself was unapproved by everyone apart from the two most involved.

Regardless of what they'd done, they were going to have at least her own whole-hearted support from now on, she decided, listening with half an ear to the organ music. First of all, though, she had to persuade the pair of them to tell the truth. It would surely be less hurtful in the long run than any supposed miscarriage.

A sudden swelling of sound announced the arrival of the bride. Scott rose unhurriedly to his feet, tall and handsome in his charcoal-grey. Worn as something of a gesture to his parents' tastes rather than to suit his own, Claire reckoned, which was something.

Jill looked radiant. Taking the tiny bouquet of miniature roses from her, Claire felt tears prickling her eyelids. In a few minutes she would be the only Marcroft left—of their particular family branch, at any rate.

'Be happy, love,' she whispered.

The ceremony seemed to take no time at all. As there were no steps into the vestry, Mr Laxton was able to wheel himself there in his electrically controlled chair. Ross moved to Claire's side as the bride and groom signed the register, setting her heart racing with that slow smile of his.

'All over bar the shouting,' he commented. 'Now we can get on with our own lives. What do you have planned for this evening?'

'Nothing,' she said simply, and saw the smile grow.

'You do now.'

His mother was watching the two of them, Claire realised. Her expression was difficult to read.

'You made an excellent job of Jill's dress,' she commented. 'If dress is wholly the right word!'

Claire glanced across at her sister, standing so tall and lovely at her new husband's side. Her hair had been scooped up in a twisted crown, to clear the stand-away collar of the coat-dress which nipped in to a slender waist before cutting sharply away to reveal the tapered lines of the trousers underneath. One of her best efforts yet, she had to acknowledge.

'Jill wanted something different,' she said.

'It's all of that, and admirable with it.' Ellen was obviously genuine in her praise. 'You really should do more with such a talent.'

Easy to say, thought Claire wryly, thanking her, not so easy to do. Finishing the design course would be a step in the right direction, but there was little hope of doing so without selling up and using the money to see her through, and that was far too much of a gamble. She was lucky to have what she'd got. Why tempt providence?

'Just family and close friends' seemed to have expanded to take in fifty or more when they got back to the house. A substantial buffet had been laid ready in the wide and gracious dining-room, with tables and chairs set out on the terrace for those who preferred to eat in the sunshine. Champagne abounded. Claire accepted a glass from a young man who introduced himself as one of the Meerston cousins.

'Related on the female side,' he added, as if she might not be capable of working that out for herself. 'How come your sister is so much taller than you?'

Claire kept the smile on her face. 'My mother was shorter than my father.'

He laughed. 'Ask a stupid question!'

'Ill-advised, at any rate,' said Ross, having come up unbeknown to either of them. He laid a light arm across Claire's shoulders, drawing sudden speculation to the other man's eyes. 'Come and meet my grandmother. She's champing at the bit.'

Claire had seen the smartly dressed, beautifully coiffured woman in church, but wouldn't have considered her anywhere near old enough to be Hugh Laxton's mother. Eyes still sharp and clear bespoke a mind equally so.

'Your sister and my grandson should both be ashamed of themselves,' she declared, 'but I don't suppose they are. How do you feel about this baby they're having?'

Claire bit her lip, conscious of Ross at her side and hating the situation Jill and Scott had placed her in. 'I was hardly delighted,' she said, on as even a note as she could manage. 'Not that my feelings one way or another make any difference.'

'You think your sister will make a good mother?'

'Don't all women when the time comes?' Claire prevaricated.

'Not necessarily. I wasn't all that good at it myself—even with a live-in nanny to take care of all the humdrum aspects.'

'Perhaps that was the reason,' suggested Claire, registering the hint of humour. 'Not enough to do.'

'Claire believes in plain speaking too, Nonna,' put in Ross on a dry note. 'You should get along fine.'

The glance turned his way was shrewd. 'We'll see.'

'Why do you call her "Nonna"?' asked Claire when they moved away.

He grinned. 'She considers the Italian version of grandmother far less aging. I'm assuming you've no grandparents of your own left either?' he added, as if the thought had just struck him.

Claire shook her head. 'My father's parents died years ago, so I never really knew them.' She did her best to keep her tone level. 'Mom's parents—Gran and Grandad—were in the car with Mom and Dad.'

They were passing a door. Ross drew her through into another smaller room, empty at present, and held her close for a moment. 'You really have gone through it,' he said roughly. 'It's a wonder you didn't go to pieces completely.'

'Don't make me into any tragedy queen,' she begged. 'Even worse things happen to some people.'

'I can't imagine much worse.' He cupped her face between his hands, looking down at her with heart-stirring tenderness. 'You need some stability putting back in your life. If——'

Someone put their head round the door, made a brief apology and vanished again, but the moment was ruined. Ross let her go, shaking his head ruefully. 'This isn't the time *or* the place. Let's go and mingle.'

Claire did so with mixed feelings. Whatever he had been about to say back there, it was no use to her if it was only based on compassion. She needed him to love her in the same way as she loved him, regardless of everything else.

They got split up after a few minutes, although she kept catching glimpses of him chatting with various people. Striking as always, in bright, singing yellow, Diane rescued her from one particularly boring individual who seemed to think he was the answer to every maiden's prayer.

'Roger never could understand that not all women are interested in his sporting exploits,' she said. 'Apart from that, how's it going?'

'Fine,' Claire confirmed. 'Couldn't be better. Mrs Laxton did a wonderful job.'

'You mean the caterers did.' There was no malice in the statement. 'I've heard at least five people making enquiries as to who made Jill's outfit. Ellen says you not only made it but designed it too. I wouldn't mind you having a go at something for me.'

'I really don't have enough time to accept commissions,' Claire returned regretfully. 'The shop has to have first priority.'

'So put in someone to run it for you, and start doing what you're obviously cut out for. You'll make a lot more.'

Claire lifted her shoulders. 'Nice thought but hardly practical,' she said wryly. 'I need to be able to rely on a regular income.'

'A few recommendations would soon see to that. I know any number who'd be only to delighted to have you design for them.' Diane was obviously unaccustomed to taking no for an answer. 'Starting with me, of course. I always have difficulty finding ready-mades that fit top and bottom equally well. Big breasts might give some men with a mother-fixation a thrill, but they're ruination when it comes to classy dressing, believe me!'

Claire was laughing, liking her all the more for her ability to turn a joke on herself. 'All right, you made your point. I'll get down some preliminary ideas, then we'll discuss it. Just you, though.'

The older woman put on her blandest expression. 'Anything you say.'

The bride and groom were nowhere to be seen—probably out on the terrace, Claire surmised. Making

her way there herself, she came across Mr Laxton, settled
in a corner of the drawing-room in his chair, with no
one paying him overmuch attention. He did indeed look
a great deal better than the first time she had seen him,
she thought. Perhaps the medics were being a little too
pessimistic in their prognosis.

'I'm so sorry you had to be put through all this,' she
said impulsively, slipping into a seat at his side. 'It should
never have happened.'

He gave her a look reminiscent of his mother's. 'All
water under the bridge now.'

It wasn't, but she had no intention of being the one
to tell him so. That had to be up to Scott and Jill themselves. The slurring in his speech was hardly noticeable
now, and he could move the formerly paralysed arm a
little, she noted. Altogether an improvement, but it still
left the heart condition to worry about.

'At least we had a lovely day for it,' she said a little
desperately. 'It just goes to show that it isn't just the
righteous the sun shines on. They do love one another,
I'm sure.'

'Evidently.' The tone was droll. 'Just a little short on
forethought.' His lips twitched as he registered her change
of expression. 'Like generations before you, yours tends
to believe itself the first to discover sexual pleasure. I'd
have expected better judgement from a son of mine,
that's all. I doubt if you'd find Ross leaving anything
to chance.' His glance shifted beyond her. 'Isn't that
right?'

'Isn't what right?' asked his elder son easily, joining
them.

'That you would always be more careful than your
brother.'

'Generally speaking, I'd hope so. Anyway,' he added
quizzically, 'what brought my name into it?'

'Your father was telling me how much he appreciates you,' said Claire, tongue in cheek, and drew a chuckle from the man in the chair.

'I've a feeling there's more to you than meets the eye,' he observed. 'Did you come to take her away, Ross?'

'Only if she's ready to go.'

'I'm not,' declared Claire truthfully. 'But do feel free to join us, if you like.'

'Well, thank you, ma'am!' Ross drew up a high-backed chair and straddled it, looking at his father with a lift of his brow. 'Sassy, isn't she?'

'Every inch,' came the bland agreement. 'Needs putting in her place, I'd say.'

'Problem is keeping her there.'

'That shouldn't be so difficult. You're bigger than she is.'

'You haven't seen her explode.'

'You two missed your vocation.' Claire was too taken up with the rapport between father and son to mind the baiting. 'You're a regular double act!'

Two pairs of identical grey eyes exchanged glances, the message obviously clear to them if not to her. The older man's nod seemed to signify approval. Of what, Claire could only guess. With Ross so close that one grey-clad knee was only bare inches from hers, she was hard put to it to maintain any composure at all. She could hardly wait for the evening, when they would be on their own again.

Ellen Laxton came up, the smile she bestowed on Claire warm and friendly. She looked very elegant in the gold suit. 'You three look very cosy,' she commented.

'Family get-together,' said her husband. 'You might point the missing members in my direction before they leave.'

'That won't be for a while yet. Their flight down to Heathrow isn't until eight-thirty.'

'Scott has been tossing back champagne as if it were going out of production,' he observed. 'I hope he isn't thinking of driving.' ·

'There's a taxi coming at half-past six,' Ross assured him. 'Everything is taken care of; don't worry.'

'I think I'll go and find somewhere a little quieter for the next hour or so, then,' he said.

'And we,' declared Ross, standing up and turning to Claire, 'will go and find your sister and her husband. I don't think you've had a chance to speak more than two words to them since we got back here.'

'Remind them that they still have to cut the cake,' said his mother. 'If they don't do it soon, they'll probably not get round to it at all.'

'In which case, you'll just have to do it for them.' Light though it was, the remark implied that there were more important things to think about. 'Claire?'

She stood up, sliding her hand into the one held out to her without looking in Ellen's direction. 'See you later then, Mr Laxton.'

Hand still clasping hers, Ross threaded a way through the throng, which seemed to have grown, if anything, over the last hour or so. Claire was conscious of the glances directed their way, of the lifted brows when people realised whom he had in tow. It was hardly surprising, considering the short time they had been acquainted, she supposed. Everyone here must know the reason for all the haste. What they wouldn't have been expecting was to see her and Ross hitting it off too.

They found Jill and Scott on the terrace amid a small crowd of their own age group. Lucy, Claire noted, appeared to be getting along famously with the best man.

'Who wants cake?' asked Scott, with champagne-stoked *bonhomie*, when passed the message from his mother. Arm about his giggling bride's shoulders, he lifted his glass to the sky. 'Here's to the two of us!'

'You mean three,' prompted someone slyly, and received a laughing glance.

'Want to bet?'

Claire felt the hand still clasping hers tighten suddenly as the implication went home, felt Ross's glance shift fleetingly to her face, and could do nothing to stop the tell-tale colour. Catching his brother's eye, Scott gave him a cheery salute.

'Too late this time, old chap. The deed is done.'

Expression stony, Ross turned on his heel and walked away, retaining his grasp on Claire's hand so that she was forced to go with him. Not that she would have thought of refusing, in any case, regardless of what she knew was coming. It had to be faced some time.

He took her to the same room that they had been in earlier—a study, she saw now, registering the antique desk and well-filled bookcases. This time he closed the door against intrusion, standing with his back to it to view her with eyes from which every vestige of warmth had been wiped.

'You were in on it too!' he declared. 'You knew the whole time!'

Had he given her the benefit of even half a doubt she would have attempted to tell him the truth of the matter, but the accusation allowed her no leeway. The anger that blitzed her obliterated all other emotions.

'So what of it?' she snapped back.

He looked at her as if he'd never really seen her before, the skin about his mouth stretched taut by the constriction of his jaw. 'You let those two put my father through all this for nothing!' he gritted. 'Damn you, Claire! I could kill you for that alone!'

She swallowed hard on the dry lump in her throat, only too aware of having burned her boats with that overhasty retort. He would never believe her now, even if she tried to retract.

'Perhaps if you hadn't interfered with Scott's life before he wouldn't have felt the need to go so far in the first place,' she said bitterly. 'He knew you'd do everything you could to stop him marrying Jill—the same way you did with that other girl. Can you deny it?'

'If I had tried to stop it, it would have been for the same reason as before—because I didn't believe him in any way ready for long-term commitment. I don't still. Especially with someone like your sister.'

'He's darn lucky to have her at all!' Claire flashed. 'She merits better herself than to be tied to an indolent wastrel! If you——' She broke off, heart plummeting sickeningly at the realisation of what was happening. 'This is getting us nowhere,' she said thickly. 'Ross, it wasn't quite the way you think. I didn't——'

'You already admitted it.' The lean features were contemptuous. 'Don't try wriggling out of it now. I'm beginning to realise just how devious you are. When you realised I was attracted to you, you decided to play for a full house, didn't you? A clever game, I'll grant you. I was convinced you were genuine.'

'I was—I am!' Claire couldn't credit what he appeared to be intimating. 'You can't possibly believe it was all an act the other night!'

'All of it, no. I give myself that much credit. As to it being your first time...' He let it go at that, watching the hot colour wash over her face with another twist of his lip. 'I think we'd better get back to the party. We both have a role still to play.'

Face pale now, Claire made no further attempt to reason with him. If he thought so little of her that he considered her capable of playing the kind of game that he was suggesting, then he could go to the devil, she told herself hollowly.

She stalked out ahead of him when he held open the door, pinning a smile to her lips as Neil Slater hove into view.

'Hi, you two,' he said. 'Been stealing a few minutes on your own? Can't say I blame you.'

'Claire has to go and help Jill change for travelling,' said Ross smoothly. 'Let's you and I find a drink.'

Neil looked from one to the other uncertainly, obviously recognising something in the atmosphere.

Claire didn't wait to hear any questions, taking herself off with a brief wave of her hand. There would come a time, she knew, when the numbness she felt right now would start to fade, but for the moment it was enough to keep her going. There was the rest of the day to get through.

CHAPTER TWELVE

THE bride and groom were cutting the cake in the dining-room, with a photographer standing by to record the event. Claire beckoned to Jill as soon as they were finished.

'It's time you thought about changing,' she said. 'The taxi will be here in half an hour.'

'Come on up with me,' the younger girl invited. 'It's going to be our last time on our own together. Scott's not bothering to change until we get to the hotel.' She giggled. 'He'll want something a bit more his style for tonight when we go out.'

'Won't it be rather late to start thinking about going out by the time you get there?' asked Claire, and received a patronising glance.

'Nothing even gets started down there before eleven! Surely you know that?'

Claire didn't, because she had never spent any time in London—let alone the Maldives. Neither had Jill, if it came to that. Her sister was going to be experiencing a whole new way of life this next week or two but she felt no envy, only a kind of sadness. The A level results would be due by the time she and Scott returned, for what they were worth—university no longer figured in her future.

Jill's going-away outfit of a pale apricot jacket and short, short skirt in orange plaid had come from a local boutique that catered for the rather more trendy end of the market. Not to Claire's taste, but then she wasn't the one wearing it.

After racking her brains, she had finally settled on matching sets of luggage as a wedding-gift. Hardly original, she knew, but they had both seemed pleased enough.

Both sets were packed and waiting to go, in the room they were to share on their return—a freshly and beautifully decorated room, big enough to take a sitting area in addition to the bed and wall-length wardrobes, and with its own bathroom.

'Nice, isn't it?' said Jill, looking about her with satisfaction. 'Have you seen the view?'

Claire duly admired it. 'You obviously don't mind coming back here to live,' she observed.

'Oh, it's only until we find somewhere of our own. There'll be plenty of time to start thinking about it when we do get back.' She hesitated before tagging on slowly, 'I suppose Ross will feel bound to spill the beans. Not a bad thing, really. They'll have got used to it by the time we're due home. Scott didn't mean to do it quite like that, of course. He's a bit tipsy.'

More than a bit, Claire would have said, but she let it pass. There seemed little point in discussing the matter any further. The damage was already done.

'Ross will take care of it,' she agreed, steeling herself against the ache. 'Are you ready? It's almost half-past.'

If there had been any genuine concern at all, it was dismissed immediately. 'You bet I am! This is going to be the most fantastic time I ever had in my whole life!'

Claire didn't doubt it. She only hoped that the honeymoon period would last a little longer than a couple of weeks.

Things moved quickly after that. In no time at all, it seemed, she was waving at the disappearing taxi from the front steps, along with a whole crowd of well-wishers. Finding Ross only feet away when she turned to go back indoors caused her heart to leap in sudden hope, but there was nothing in his expression to suggest a change of view—an impression confirmed by his cold tone.

'Dad would like a word with you, if you can spare a few minutes. You'll find him in the study.'

Green eyes widened. 'You've told him already?'

'It seemed best to get it over with as soon as possible.'

'Best for whom?' she asked with asperity. 'Couldn't he be allowed at least a few days' peace?'

The rest of the party had returned inside, leaving the two of them alone, one at the top, one at the bottom of the broad stone steps. From this angle Ross looked taller than ever, his hands thrust into trouser pockets, shoulders squared.

'I think *you'd* best keep your opinions to yourself,' he said tautly. 'Are you going to talk to him, or doesn't your nerve stretch that far?'

Hair fired by the lowering sun at her back, eyes blazing, Claire let rip, beyond caring what she said. 'Stop being so damned self-righteous! You're more to blame than anybody for all this! You're so full of yourself, Ross. You even thought you'd got *me* grovelling at your feet! Well, I've got news for you. I don't grovel. Neither do I evade. I'll talk to your father any time!'

Ross looked at her calculatingly for a lengthy moment, then shook his head as if dismissing whatever notion had occurred. 'As I said, you'll find him in the study.'

He made no move to stand aside when she came up the steps, leaving her no alternative but to brush past him in the doorway. Every fibre of her anticipated some physical retaliation, but it didn't come, although she could feel the anger radiating from him.

His control made her ashamed of her own lack of it. She couldn't even recall all she'd said just now, only the viciousness of the delivery. Not that anything she'd said could make things any worse than they already were. Whatever Ross's feelings had been before, there was no doubting what they were now. Total abhorrence about summed it up.

Hugh Laxton was alone in the study, his chair by the window. He looked across at her steadily.

'Close the door,' he instructed. 'Let's have a little privacy.' He indicated a nearby chair when she had complied. 'Come and sit down. We need to sort this thing out.'

Claire took the seat, observing his lack of obvious distress with relief. There had been no cause for Ross to be quite so precipitate all the time.

'Ross tells me I'm not going to be a grandfather after all,' he said, surprisingly mildly. 'I can't say I'm all that sorry. Whether Ellen will feel the same I'm not so sure. She'd begun making plans.' He paused, studying her, the still-handsome face not unfriendly. 'Did you really know about it from the first?'

Claire shook her head. 'I only found out a few days ago. There didn't seem a lot I could do about it at that stage.'

'I doubt if there was much you could have done at any stage. Scott was always headstrong. So is Ross, if not in quite the same way. Why did you let him think you were in on the conspiracy—if that's not too strong a word?'

'I saw red when he accused me of it,' she admitted wryly. 'He didn't give me a chance to explain.'

'As I said, headstrong. You too, it appears. Are you going to give it another try?'

'There wouldn't be any point. He wouldn't believe me. We're about as alienated as two people can be.'

'But do you want to stay that way?'

She lifted her shoulders, unwilling to reveal too much. 'It isn't important.'

'Considering the way you were together earlier, I'd have said it very important. I've met Ross's women-friends in the past, but never one he looked at the way he looked at you. I believe you feel the same way about him, too.'

'It isn't confined to the male,' Claire admitted, and saw a faint smile come and go.

'It's more than mere lust, for certain. I'm capable of recognising that much. I thought he'd finally found the right one. I still do think so. If you let this ruin things for you, you'll both live to regret it.'

'The one thing I do regret is not keeping a better eye on my sister,' she said, turning a deaf ear to the rest. 'I'm sorry for all the trouble it's caused you. It was the last thing you needed at a time like this.'

'If you mean because of my condition, I'm far more resilient than might be imagined.' He inclined his head as her expression altered. 'Yes, I know the prognosis. Medical opinion has been proved wrong before. With Ross taking all the pressure, I aim to live a few more years yet.' The pause was brief. 'You won't change your mind and talk to him again?'

'It wouldn't be any good. He doesn't want to know.'

'I'd knock both your heads together if I could get out of this damned chair!' Hugh sounded exasperated. 'Intractability is no virtue. You'll have to accept a lift home from him at the very least, having come in the limousine.'

'I'll call a taxi,' she said, getting to her feet. On impulse, she bent and put her lips to one thin cheek. 'Thanks, anyway, for taking it all so well. I'd never have forgiven myself if you'd suffered any ill effects.'

'My son and your sister would have been to blame if I had, not you,' came the bluff reply. 'Don't let what's happened between you and Ross keep you away.'

The possibility of Ross walking in on any such visit made it unlikely that she would take up the invitation, but she let it stand. Ellen might not be so keen, anyway, not when she knew.

Departures were already under way, she found on leaving the study. The Johnsons had been looking for her. A taxi was already on its way, it appeared. Was she going to come back with them?

Agreeing, Claire went to find Ellen, summoning a smile as she thanked her for all she had done. There was no sign of Ross, thank heaven.

'I took it that you'd be staying on for the evening,' said the older woman on a surprised note. 'Ross planned on taking a small group over to the country club. I'm sure you were included.'

Claire gave a rueful shrug. 'I think it would be better if you heard the reasons why I won't be staying from him. Not that I'm dressed for the country club, in any case.' She added swiftly, 'Thanks again for everything. You gave them a wonderful send-off. I'm just sorry for what you are going to hear.'

'The taxi's here,' announced Barry Johnson, coming up with his wife in tow. 'It's been a real treat, Mrs Laxton,' he added with sincerity. 'A wonderful effort all round.'

'We do our best,' she said. Her glance back at Claire revealed a certain dawning suspicion. 'Perhaps we'll see you over the weekend?'

With the Johnsons standing by, there was little else to do but smile again and nod. 'Perhaps.'

Ross was saying goodbye to some other people at the door when the three of them reached it. Claire forced herself to follow suit when Barry expressed further congratulations on a job well done, meeting the icy grey eyes with a hostility of her own. Then they were outside, and getting into the waiting taxi.

She didn't look back as they moved off down the drive.

Faced with a request for more money on Friday, her bank manager said a definite no. She was over-extended as it was for the size of the business, he pointed out. He might even have to consider reviewing the whole loan.

Claire made no mention of the increase in leasing costs for fear that he might do it there and then. For the present she would simply have to use the money she had intended Jill to have, she concluded, depressed. If she put the house on the market right away there was a chance of a sale before the summer was over; that would realise enough capital to re-finance the business *and* give Jill her dues. She could always rent a flat.

The weekend passed slowly, the week even more so. She showed three lots of people around the house on Sunday, none of whom expressed any serious interest. It was a buyer's market at present, the estate agent told her. They could pick and choose.

By the following Saturday, with no contact from the Laxtons, or even Diane, she had reached a stage where nothing much seemed to touch her.

It took Jill's phone call to the shop to announce their return home to jerk Claire out of her apathy. Her sister sounded full of the joys of living, eager to show off her tan and all the photographs they'd taken over the two weeks. They'd be coming over that evening, she said.

Jill would have to come down to earth some time, thought Claire, and just hoped it wouldn't be with as hard a bump as she had experienced herself.

By half-past eight she was beginning to think that they weren't coming after all. The easiest way to find out was to phone the Laxton house, but she couldn't bring herself to do it. The sound of a car turning into the drive around nine brought her to her feet in relief.

She should have expected Jill to have forgotten to bring her key, she thought fondly when the bell was pressed. The welcoming smile froze on her lips when she found Ross on the doorstep instead.

Wearing a dinner-suit, he looked like every woman's dream escort, but there was nothing dreamlike about his expression. He wasted no time on any greeting.

'I'm afraid there's been an accident. I've come to take you to the hospital. Scott rang from there. He's relatively unhurt, but Jill has to undergo surgery.' He spread his hands in a gesture of apology. 'That's all I know as yet.'

Claire gazed at him with eyes wide and dark in the sudden pallor of her face. Not again, she thought numbly. Please, not again!

'She's alive,' Ross said gently, sensing what was going through her mind. 'Hang on to that.' He indicated the waiting car. 'We can be there in fifteen minutes.'

Claire forced her limbs into movement, feeling as if they were no longer a part of her. Some remaining shred of rationality bade her take up the doorkey before leaving the house, but she didn't stop to don a jacket over her thin cotton shirt. The fear of what they were going to find ate into every crevice of her brain. Jill was all she had left. If she died...

Ross opened the car door for her and saw her into the seat, fastening the belt across her himself when her fingers fumbled it. He offered no further verbal solicitude, for which she was grateful. Right now she couldn't have taken it.

'How did it happen?' she got out, when they were on the road.

Ross shook his head. 'They were on their way over here. That's as much as I can tell you.'

'It will be your brother's fault!' she accused bitterly. 'He drives like a madman!'

Ross kept his eyes on the road, his tone steady. 'Let's leave the accusations until we know the full story.'

He was the last one to preach, came the fleeting thought, pushed aside as fear closed in on her once more. Nothing mattered except Jill. Nothing!

Joining Scott in the small side-room reserved for anxious relatives some fifteen minutes later, Claire made every effort to control her initial impulses. The pallor that came with shock had turned his tan sallow, although the only visible signs of physical injury were a collar about his neck and his arm in a sling.

'It's been more than an hour already,' he said dully. 'If she doesn't——' He broke off, raising a face from which every vestige of spirit had been drained. 'It will be my fault. It was all my fault. I was driving too fast. We went off the road—turned over. Jill took the brunt of it. If she dies I'll kill myself! I shan't *want* to live without her.'

Claire forced back the words trembling on her lips, and said instead, 'She isn't going to die. She's young and strong. She'll pull through, I know she will!'

Ross moved abruptly. 'I'll go and find out what's happening.'

The door opened as he turned to it, to admit the senior nurse who had shown them in there. She was smiling, obviously happy to be able to relay good news.

'It hasn't turned out to be quite as bad as first feared,' she announced. 'Several broken ribs, severe bruising, some internal injury—but nothing critical. Given her youth, she should be up and about again in next to no time.'

'When can we see her?' asked Claire, hardly able to contain the tears of sheer relief.

'She'll be out for quite a while yet, so it would probably be best if you left it till the morning.'

'I'm staying anyway,' declared Scott adamantly. 'I want to be there when she does wake up.'

Claire started to say that she would stay too, caught Ross's eye and let the words fade. Fault or no fault, Scott was the one whom Jill would most want to see on opening her eyes. At the very least, there was no doubting the depth of his feelings for her any more; he looked like a man who had been given a new lease of life. Hopefully, he had a new outlook to go with it too.

'I'll get a taxi back,' she said in the lift. 'You can go on to wherever it was you were going—if it's not too late.'

'Chamber of Commerce dinner,' Ross supplied, with the intimation that it wasn't important enough to merit any concern. 'I'll drive you home myself.'

Claire watched the descending numbers, throat dry and aching. 'I'd as soon not, thanks.'

He made no answer, just waited until they were outside, then took her arm and marched her across to where he had left the car. She went with only minimal protest, too drained for any greater effort. Jill was going to be all right; that was the main thing.

She couldn't even summon the willpower to say anything when he turned into the drive on reaching the house and switched off the ignition, with the obvious intention of seeing her indoors.

'I'll make some coffee,' he said in the hall. 'You go and sit down.'

She went because her legs felt like jelly—delayed shock, she assumed. It was still only a little after ten-thirty, she saw disbelievingly. It felt as though half the night had passed since Ross had turned up on the doorstep.

He had taken off both jacket and tie when he brought the coffee through, his white dress shirt open at the throat. Claire steeled herself not to show any reaction as her fingers brushed his on taking the cup from him. Nothing had changed; he still set her senses alight even now.

'Drink it,' he commanded when she made to put the cup down after a token sip. 'It's hot and it's sweet. Good for shock if nothing else.'

'I'm all right,' she insisted. 'It was good of you to make it, but I really don't need it. She added huskily, 'Thanks for coming to tell me. Hearing it over the phone would have been far worse.'

'The least I could do.' Still standing, Ross wasn't drinking his coffee either. 'I'd say Scott did a whole lot of growing up tonight. I'm just sorry it had to happen this way.'

'Do your parents know yet?'

'I rang while I was waiting for the kettle to boil. They're only too thankful it isn't any worse.'

'How did your mother take the news about the baby?' she felt bound to ask.

'Rather badly at first, but she's managed to adjust.'

The pause stretched for several seconds after that. Claire looked steadfastly down at the cup still in her hand, wishing he would go and dreading the moment when he did at one and the same time. She hadn't expected to see him alone again ever.

When Ross did move, it was with deliberation—taking the cup from her hand and placing it on the coffee-table, then drawing her up and into his arms. Claire returned the kiss honestly, hungrily, not attempting to work out the whys and wherefores. It was enough, for the moment, to be close to him again.

'Dad said you told him you only discovered there was no pregnancy a few days before the wedding,' he said on a roughened note some moments later, still holding her. 'If that's true, why did you let me think otherwise?'

'Because you were already convinced of it,' she got out. 'I wasn't going to start pleading innocence when you'd already made up your mind that I'd been lying through my teeth the whole time. I was devastated when I did find out the truth, but I didn't know what to do about it.'

'You could have told me.'

'And then what? Have you try to get the wedding stopped?'

'It would have been a bit late for that.'

'So there was no point in my telling you, was there?' She put up a shaky hand to brush back a recalcitrant lock of copper hair, looking up at him with appeal in her eyes. 'I thought it best to at least get the wedding over without any further upset. Especially after all the trouble your mother had already gone to.'

Ross searched her features, his expression difficult to read. 'And afterwards?'

'It would have had to come out some time, of course. I just didn't expect Scott to do it the way he did.'

The smile was faint. 'He did it to poke me in the eye. Retaliation for the times I *have* managed to put a stop to his schemes. Not that I can lay the blame for my re-action at his door. I jumped to too many wrong conclusions.'

'Does that mean you don't believe I had any ulterior motive where you're concerned any more?' she asked, trying not to leap too far ahead herself.

'It means,' he said ruefully, 'that I've spent the last two weeks in a hole mostly of my own digging.'

'I did a little digging of my own, if it comes to that,' Claire acknowledged. 'One of these days I might learn to stop my tongue from running away with me!'

'About the same time hell freezes over.' Ross was smiling genuinely now, hands about her neck, fingertips caressing her nape. 'You wouldn't be you if you stopped to consider before you reacted. I'll just have to re-member not to ignite the touch-paper too often.'

He was igniting it right this minute—sending her pulse-rate into overdrive. Claire parted her lips when he kissed her again, giving free rein to the emotions crowding her.

Without taking his mouth from hers, he lifted her and sat down with her on the sofa, much as he had that first evening at the flat, holding her across his lap with her head in the crook of his arm. His free hand sought and found her breast within the thin shirt she was wearing, his touch tenderly possessive.

'No more misunderstandings,' he said softly. 'I love you, Green-eyes. More than I thought it possible to love any woman.'

'Are you sure you're not confusing it with something else?' she whispered, still not wholly convinced.

He laughed and shook his head. 'There's no confusion. Not where I'm concerned. I've spent years looking for the one woman I'd want to spend the rest of my life with. I'd almost given up hope. I suppose I should be grateful that Scott is the way he is. If he and Jill hadn't got together, we might never have met.'

There was a pause as he studied her, his expression undergoing a subtle alteration. 'I realise you might not feel as much for me just yet, but...'

Claire placed her fingers against his lips, staying the words. Her face was soft and glowing, her eyes like twin stars. 'I feel just as much, if not more,' she claimed, certain at last. 'I have for ages!'

The lean features relaxed again, mouth slowly widening. 'You haven't known me ages.'

'Days, weeks—what does it matter? I was bowled over the moment you walked through the door.'

'Until I dropped the bombshell on you.'

'Even then, if I'm honest,' she admitted. 'Much as I tried to persuade myself that I hated you.'

'I was pretty brutal,' Ross agreed ruefully. 'And not only that time either. Not that you didn't ask for what you got when you slapped me in the face,' he added, with a sudden spark in his eyes at the memory. 'You pack quite a punch for a featherweight.'

Claire laughed, no longer caring about her lack of stature. Ross loved her; that made her feel ten feet tall anyway. 'I think you won that round on points.'

'A draw at any rate.' He drew her up to him, kissing her with a tenderness more telling than any words. 'I want to take care of you,' he murmured against her lips.

'From now on, your problems are my problems. Tomorrow we start sorting out your finances.'

'I don't want money from you,' she protested. 'I love *you*, Ross, not what you're worth!'

'You'd hardly expect me to let my wife struggle along trying to make ends meet,' he declared on a firmer note. 'In any case, selling isn't really what you want to do most, is it? Diane said you already agreed to design for her. You could devote yourself full time to that side of things and let the shop go.'

His wife. It sounded wonderful, but she wasn't ready to have him take her over lock, stock and barrel.

'I'm not good enough for that,' she said.

'Yes, you are. According to Diane, there'd be no shortage of takers. She was dubious about contacting you after I admitted that the two of us weren't exactly on friendly terms any more. She'll be highly relieved we made it up—and not just for the sake of her wardrobe either. She likes you.'

'I like her too.' Claire stirred restlessly. 'All the same...'

Ross shook his head. 'We can discuss all that later. Right now there are more important things to think about. I'm staying the night. If you want me to I'll sleep in the guest-room, but I'm not leaving you on your own in the house after the shock you've had.'

'More than one,' she returned softly, abandoning the argument for the present. She brought up her hand to trace the hard-boned lines of his face, her eyes darkening as the hunger intensified. 'To hell with the guest-room! I want you, Ross.'

His laugh was low. 'Anything you say, darling.'

For now at any rate, she thought with a flash of humour as he gathered her up to get to his feet. Tomorrow was a whole new day.

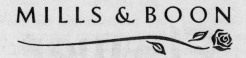

MILLS & BOON

Next Month's Romances

Each month you can choose from a wide variety of romance with Mills & Boon. Below are the new titles to look out for next month.

CLIMAX OF PASSION	Emma Darcy
MARRYING MARY	Betty Neels
EARTHBOUND ANGEL	Catherine George
A WEEKEND TO REMEMBER	Miranda Lee
HOLLYWOOD WEDDING	Sandra Marton
COMING HOME	Patricia Wilson
A CAREFUL WIFE	Lindsay Armstrong
FAST AND LOOSE	Elizabeth Oldfield
CHARLOTTE'S COWBOY	Jeanne Allan
SISTER OF THE BRIDE	Valerie Parv
ONE-NIGHT WIFE	Day Leclaire
HEARTLESS STRANGER	Elizabeth Duke
DANGEROUS GROUND	Alison Kelly
TENDER CAPTIVE	Rosemary Carter
BRIDE OF MY HEART	Rebecca Winters
TOO LATE FOR REGRETS	Liza Hadley

Fl wer P wer

How would you like to win a year's supply of simply irresistible romances? Well, you can and they're free! Simply unscramble the words below and send the completed puzzle to us by 31st August 1996. The first 5 correct entries picked after the closing date will win a years supply of Temptation novels (four books every month—worth over £100).

1	LTIUP	TULIP
2	FIDLADFO	
3	ERSO	
4	AHTNYHCI	
5	GIBANOE	
6	NEAPUTI	
7	YDSIA	
8	SIIR	
9	NNAIATCRO	
10	LDIAAH	
11	RRSEOIMP	
12	LEGXFOOV	
13	OYPPP	
14	LZEAAA	
15	COIRDH	

Please turn over for details of how to enter ☞

Hw to enter

Listed overleaf are 15 jumbled-up names of flowers. All you have to do is unscramble the names and write your answer in the space provided. We've done the first one for you!

When you have found all the words, don't forget to fill in your name and address in the space provided below and pop this page into an envelope (you don't need a stamp) and post it today. Hurry—competition ends 31st August 1996.

Mills & Boon Flower Puzzle
FREEPOST
Croydon
Surrey
CR9 3WZ

Are you a Reader Service Subscriber?   Yes ☐   No ☐

Ms/Mrs/Miss/Mr _____

Address _____

_____

_____ Postcode _____

One application per household.

You may be mailed with other offers from other reputable companies as a result of this application. If you would prefer not to receive such offers, please tick box. ☐

COMP396
B